His BlackBerry chirped

"Derrick Cavenaugh."

"Mr. Cavenaugh, this is Detective Oaks with the Atherton PD. I'm at the Stop Right on the corner of Elm and Matteson. There's been an incident with your daughter, Leslie, and I'm afraid the owner intends to press charges...."

Derrick pasted on a calm expression, while his insides churned up the take-out sushi he'd gulped down for lunch. But as the cop summed up Leslie's latest contribution to Derrick's plunge into single-parent insanity, Derrick kept his panic to himself. He was getting good at it.

His oldest had apparently skipped classes again. And now she had her sights firmly set on adding a petty larceny conviction to her middle school résumé.

Dear Reader,

Success can be a fickle goal to chase. For some of us, the reality of life never quite lives up to the promise of our youth. And yet there's a wonderful sort of starting over that can happen when we break free of expectation. When we start saying what's next, instead of looking back.

High school valedictorian Bailey Greenwood never made it to college, and All-American quarterback Derrick Cavenaugh washed out long before realizing his dream of playing pro ball. But these two fighters are everything champions should be—whether they're ready to believe it or not. And their journeys have brought them to the same place. They can continue to define themselves by past failures, or they can start fighting for the new dreams just beyond their reach.

Participating in the SINGLES...WITH KIDS series has been a blast. This isn't my first single-parent story, but it's turned out to be my favorite. Each of the books in SINGLES...WITH KIDS is uplifting, heartwarming and at times laugh-out-loud funny. And the same message rings throughout: single parents are hardworking, determined survivors, and they are champions, one and all.

So to all the single moms and dads fighting and dreaming out there, let me just say—well done!

I love to hear from readers. Please let me know what you think of my stories at www.annawrites.com. And join the fun and fabulous giveaways at annadestefano.blogspot.com.

Sincerely,

Anna

ALL-AMERICAN
FATHER
Anna DeStefano

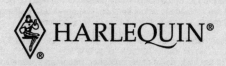

TORONTO • NEW YORK • LONDON
AMSTERDAM • PARIS • SYDNEY • HAMBURG
STOCKHOLM • ATHENS • TOKYO • MILAN • MADRID
PRAGUE • WARSAW • BUDAPEST • AUCKLAND

ISBN-13: 978-0-373-71410-0
ISBN-10:   0-373-71410-6

ALL-AMERICAN FATHER

This edition published by arrangement with Harlequin Books S.A.

® and TM are trademarks of the publisher. Trademarks indicated with
® are registered in the United States Patent and Trademark Office, the
Canadian Trade Marks Office and in other countries.

www.eHarlequin.com

Printed in U.S.A.

ABOUT THE AUTHOR

Romantic Times BOOKreviews award-winning author Anna DeStefano fell in love at first sight with her hero husband. Watching him become the world's greatest father from the first moment he held their son in his hands, she fell in love with him all over again. It's difficult for her to choose her favorite part of writing family dramas—at least until she dreams up another hardworking hero doing his very best for his family. Then it's show over. The fathers get to her every time.

Books by Anna DeStefano

HARLEQUIN SUPERROMANCE

Don't miss any of our special offers. Write to us at the following address for information on our newest releases.

Harlequin Reader Service
U.S.: 3010 Walden Ave., P.O. Box 1325, Buffalo, NY 14269
Canadian: P.O. Box 609, Fort Erie, Ont. L2A 5X3

For

Andrew
my champion,

and

Jimmy
my dream catcher.

CHAPTER ONE

"NICE JOB, CAVENAUGH." Derrick's senior partner slapped him on the shoulder as they left the high-rise conference room behind.

"Thanks, Spencer," Derrick replied with the expected hint of nonchalance. "We'll have the merger portfolio ready for Reynolds-Allied to sign by the end of the month."

It felt good to be in control of something.

Anything.

Contract law wasn't as sexy as the professional football career he and his old man had envisioned for Derrick's life. But being on top of his game during high-stakes negotiations was its own kind of rush.

The boardroom was the only place he wasn't failing on a daily basis, since returning to San Francisco a year ago. Where his—God, he hated the word—*potential* wasn't being wasted.

"You're coming to the alumni mixer at the Western–Langston game in a couple of weeks, right?" Spencer Hastings's questions were rarely just questions. Derrick was being summoned. And Hastings had a stranglehold on the junior partner promotion Derrick was banking his family's future on. "You'll make everyone's night by showing up."

"I…" Derrick's legacy as *the* alumni football star from San Francisco's Western High had secured him a spot at the firm of Hastings Chase Whitney. But he was a chronic no-show at as many local social events as he could avoid. Especially the sports-related ones, where there was little business to be done, and too much of what he was supposed to have become slapping him in the face. Like the Western alumni gathering, scheduled for Western's annual grudge match against Langston High School, this year to be played at Langston's stadium across the bay—the suburb where Derrick now lived with his girls. "I'll have to find a sitter for Leslie and Savannah."

"Nonsense." Hastings gave his shoulder a firmer slap as the elevator rushed them to the ground floor. "Bring the kids along."

Derrick tried to picture his twelve-year-old and nine-year-old, resentful already of the time his job stole from them, listening to Daddy relive glory days with a bunch of people they didn't know. In under half an hour, he'd have a Powerpuff-Girl-sized mutiny on his hands.

Zam.

Pow!

Dad, we wanna go. Now!

"I'll see what I can do." He flashed his golden-boy grin to smooth things along. "My oldest is working on a science project, and—"

His BlackBerry chirped.

He sifted through his overflowing briefcase as they emerged through revolving doors onto the bustling sidewalk.

"Derrick Cavenaugh."

"Mr. Cavenaugh, this is Detective Oaks with the Langston PD. I'm at the Stop Right on the corner of Elm and Matteson. There's been an incident with your daughter, Leslie, and I'm afraid the owner intends to press charges…."

Derrick pasted on a calm expression, while his insides churned up the take-out sushi he'd gulped down for lunch. Hastings kept his gaze politely focused on the shuffle of business people streaming by. But as the cop summed up Leslie's latest contribution to Derrick's plunge into single-parent insanity, Derrick kept his panic to himself. He was getting good at it.

His oldest had apparently skipped classes again. And now she had her sights firmly set on adding a petty larceny conviction to her middle school resume.

TWO PART-TIME JOBS…

One aging bed-and-breakfast by the bay…

A cop and a preteen thief standing between Bailey Greenwood and the end of her Stop Right shift...

Cost to Bailey's insomnia-challenged grip on reality?

Priceless.

"Mr. Drayton, I need to get going," she said. "I've already given the officer my statement, and—"

"Not until the girl's father arrives," grumped the convenience store owner who'd insisted that she cover the afternoon shift, because he'd been *unavailable* when Sally Traver called in sick. But wave the petty theft of a seven-dollar box of condoms before the cheapskate, and Drayton had beaten the police to the store. "I want the officer to have all the information he needs to put that little hoodlum behind bars."

The hoodlum in question was currently slumped in the cracked plastic chair in Drayton's office, cowering in a jailbait ensemble Bailey suspected had been purchased somewhere like Bloomingdale's, rather than the latest mall-rat hangout. The kid had attitude to spare, but she seemed more desperate for attention than becoming a hoodlum-in-training.

"She's got the money to pay for what she took." The girl had flashed an impressive wad of cash in a snotty attempt to keep Bailey from calling the cops. "Why not let her square things, then leave her parents to deal with the rest?"

And let me get to Margo's Bistro before I lose the

*new job that might spring me from this dump, if I can
get enough hours there.*

"The money's not the point," the man actually
had the nerve to say, when *bottom line* was his
native language. "If I let one of these miscreants off,
they'll be all over this place, taking me for everything I'm worth."

As if there was a gang of upper-middle-class hell-
raisers looking to supplement their allowances by
pilfering from the resident Scrooge!

Larry Drayton stocked the cheapest inventory he
could get away with selling, trading on his prime
location as the only convenience store on the main
drag that led from their affluent bedroom community
to the interstate linking them to the Golden Gate. He
was downright rude to customers, inflexible on prin-
ciple with his hourly employees and did a nimble
tightrope dance around the regulations of his trade
that would bite him in the butt one day.

Bailey had checked the expiry date on the Trojan
condoms she'd reclaimed from the kid. If their under-
aged klepto was planning a party, Bailey had done her
and the girl's parents a favor. Evidently, it had been
ten years since Scrooge last stocked prophylactics.

"I'm going to grab my things," she murmured.

Scott Fletcher had wandered in a few minutes
ago—a half hour late for his shift. She was free to
go, as soon as *Daddy* showed.

What kind of parent took an hour and a half to get himself to the scene of his child's crime?

When Bailey entered the office, the pop-princess wanna-be rearranged her worried features into a scowl. The kid's attempt at tough came off lonely and scared, the combination weakening Bailey's determination to not get involved.

She didn't have time for *involved*. But neither did this blond angel's parents, evidently.

"You know—" she slipped into Scrooge's chair "—if your guy can't spring for the rubbers, you might want to consider trading up."

The girl—Leslie, Bailey had heard her say to the cop when she'd recited her dad's cell number— looked shocked, a split second before she rebounded with a sneer.

"Like there's just one guy."

"Well, if you're going to tag-team it," Bailey smart-assed back, "I'd suggest you shoplift at the Wal-Mart. Prehistoric condoms are a bad deal, even when they're free."

The kid's forehead scrunched in confusion, morphing her toughness into the kind of adorable she shouldn't be in such a hurry to outgrow. Bailey plucked the discarded condoms from the desk and tossed them over. The girl snatched the box one-handed.

Nice reflexes.

Hopefully, her mind was just as quick.

"Condoms have expiration dates for a reason," Bailey explained. "They tend to break after they've been sitting for too long."

More scrunching, then an image of what *breaking* meant must have flashed through the girl's mind. Cheeks reddening, she glanced down at the pre-Y2K date on the box, then slapped the condoms to the desk.

"Oh…" Looking younger by the second, she clenched her hands in her lap. "I—"

"Leslie Marie Cavenaugh!" a masculine voice boomed from the doorway.

The kid's face drained of color, turning mutinous at the same time. Crossing her arms, she sank farther into the acid-green chair.

Bailey barely noticed.

Daddy was six-four and then some, with the kind of broad shoulders and trim waist that did dangerous things to a woman's fantasies. His pricey suit screamed money and privilege, but the hands braced on his hips looked as tough as ever, and his nose had been broken more than once.

Bailey had seen the first break from the sidelines. He'd thrown the winning touchdown pass at Western's 1995 state championship game, and the opposing defensive end had taken exception.

Just looking at him brought the past flooding back.

"Derrick Cavenaugh."

It took a few seconds to realize she'd said his

name out loud. Several seconds more to register that he hadn't recognized her in return.

And why on earth should he?

Western High's "Most Likely to Succeed" blinked down at her, a washed-up valedictorian, without a flicker of recognition for the woman who'd worshiped him from afar, when she hadn't been much older than his daughter.

CHAPTER TWO

SHRUGGING OFF the admiring glances of women was nothing new. Derrick was a large man who, whether he wanted to or not, enjoyed the even larger public persona that came with having been a pro football prospect. Even after his NFL dreams tanked, compliments of a near-crippling back injury, the Mighty DC still got noticed.

While married to Amanda, random female attention never tempted him to do more than look back. Since she left him for his ex-best friend, Rodney Canton, life had been too raw for Derrick to give a damn.

Until roughly sixty seconds ago.

The pixie-like woman sitting behind the shabby desk had devoured him with her eyes before he'd made it through the door. When she'd whispered his name in that husky voice, every muscle below his waist had clenched with the instinct to get closer. Soft, curly chestnut hair held back with a rubber band, a heart-shaped face completely devoid of makeup, she'd looked both familiar and different at the same time.

Though different from *what* was anyone's guess, since as far as he knew, they'd never met.

He'd bet his Reynolds-Allied bonus she wouldn't make five-two stick in heels, and his tastes usually veered toward leggy blondes with mischief in their eyes. The woman now looking everywhere *but* at him had the air of someone too harried to give mischief a second glance.

So why did he have the urge to get her on her feet to see if the waist half-hidden behind the desk was really as tiny as he imagined it would be?

"Dad!" His mortified preteen glanced between him and the stranger he'd been gaping at.

Sinking into the agony of watching his oldest daughter spiral into a dark place he couldn't protect her from, Derrick gave his fear and anger free rein.

"Get your butt in the car." He jerked his thumb over his shoulder. "There's no chance of talking the shop owner out of pressing charges, but the cop said you're sprung until you go before the judge. Do yourself a favor and work up the necessary enthusiasm to say you're sorry on the way out the door."

Before a year ago, he'd never said anything harsher than *boo* to his children. They'd been daddy's girls from birth. So eager to please, just like Amanda. He'd eaten up every smile and *I love you, Daddy,* not for a second realizing how elusive that kind of adoration could be—in both daughters and wives.

"I already said I'm sorry," Leslie mumbled. "Two hours ago, when that cop called you."

Her scowl trembled, then she tightened that traitorous lower lip that turned Derrick's heart to mush every time she fought not to cry. Staring down at the stiletto boots she'd shown up in a week ago, with no explanation of where they'd come from, she slinked out of the office like a shadow of the good kid he knew still lurked inside.

"She's crying out for attention."

Derrick whirled on the woman who'd finally risen to her feet.

"Excuse me?"

Judgment and disapproval had replaced her blatant admiration. She tucked the hem of her T-shirt into well-worn jeans no woman should look that spectacular in. Then she and the waist that was even tinier than he'd envisioned stepped around the desk.

"The longer you took to get here, the more belligerent your daughter became."

"Traffic over the bridge was a bitch, not that it's any of your business."

Bailey, or so her name badge read, twirled a tendril of hair between nervous fingers. She started to speak, stopped, then shrugged as if to say, *what the hell.*

"Your daughter's getting in over her head." She met his gaze dead-on, which took guts considering he was ready to explode and his expression no doubt showed it. "Stealing is bad enough, but—"

"I'm a lawyer. I don't need a convenience store clerk to tell me that shoplifting is a serious offense. I just got an earful from the cop outside."

"Did he bother to mention what your daughter took?" Her eyes narrowed.

"No. Stealing is stealing."

"Not if you're a twelve-year-old girl." She reached for a purse and a familiar-shaped box. "You don't remember me, Derrick, but you seemed like a pretty good guy in high school. When you find the time in your busy schedule, you or your wife might want to have a talk with Leslie about birth control."

He stared at the twelve-pack of condoms. His mouth opened to fire a dozen questions at the departing Bailey, but he couldn't find the words.

His baby girl was apparently flirting with the idea of being sexually active, and the sassy clerk at the Stop Right, the crotchety owner and even Detective Oaks had known before Derrick had.

"I KNOW I'M LATE," Bailey blurted as she hustled into Margo's Bistro.

Giving up on heading home to shower and change, she'd raced away from the Stop Right—and Derrick Cavenaugh's domestic problems—and headed straight for the bistro.

"It's slow for a Thursday night." Margo Evans motioned toward the group of women she'd been sitting with at a corner table. "A few friends popped in. Nothing Robert and I couldn't handle."

Margo and her husband's bistro had become the latest trendy meeting spot for the residents and business people who milled around San Francisco's South of Market Area. A month or so back, Bailey and Margo had bumped into each other, literally, while Bailey bussed tables and circulated trays at a wedding the other woman attended.

Margo had needed weekday help in the evenings, which was perfect for Bailey. Her hands were full at her family's bed-and-breakfast all morning. Every day. And the bistro's pay beat the minimum wage Drayton grudgingly doled out.

"Get back to your friends." Bailey slipped behind the counter. "I'll see what Robert needs."

Pushing through the double doors to the kitchen, she clocked in and grabbed her apron. *Bailey* had been embroidered in sunny yellow on the apron's apple-green fabric. As if she belonged there, when Margo's was just one more part-time job in the endless string she'd had since high school.

Dead-end jobs were necessary. They kept the bills paid. They weren't anything close to the exciting life she'd dreamed of, but that was fine. So was arriving at her second part-time gig of the day, rumpled and twelve hours past shower-fresh. Whatever she had to do, however she looked doing it, Bailey didn't mind, as long as she kept her grandmother's business afloat.

"You want to take these out while I get the ladies their drinks?" Robert handed over a plate filled with specialty muffins and scones that were typically sold out after the breakfast rush. For Margo and her friends, he'd broken into tomorrow morning's stash.

Bailey smiled and nodded, heading into the other room with the platter. Robert co-owned the bistro with Margo, and he had some big-time job in finance or banking. But nights and weekends, when he wasn't hanging out with Margo's kids, he was in the bistro lending a hand wherever she needed him. They were one part newlyweds, married just since August, and one part old married couple. The kind of couple that finished each others' sentences and slipped into both romantic and silly moments as if they'd never known any different.

Their happiness would be enchanting to watch if their ready-made family didn't reek of the kind of too-good-to-be-true situation that Bailey typically avoided.

"Here you go." She set pastries in front of her boss and the other two women at the table.

"I tell you, he's not going to come," said the brightly dressed woman beside Margo who looked vaguely familiar.

"He's in over his head." Margo's other friend managed to look both tough and gentle as she contributed to the evening's gossip.

Margo chuckled. "That's usually when most people think they have it all figured out."

"Can I get you anything else?" Bailey asked, maintaining the illusion of privacy while she stood close enough to take their next order. She was there, but she was invisible.

The service industry is in our blood, Grams kept saying, passing off the Greenwood family's legacy of perpetually serving, while others relaxed and took a break from their lives, as a magical gift bestowed upon only the chosen few.

"No, thank you, Bailey. This looks lovely." Margo smiled, as if the way Bailey had placed the plate of desserts on the table was a slice of heaven on earth.

"I'll get your drinks." Bailey backed away, her return smile forced.

She needed this job. To keep the Gables Inn out of the red, she'd take two or three more just like it. Her new employer's overly exuberant appreciation was a small cross to bear, even if it held a hint of pity for how much Bailey and her grandmother were struggling.

"Drinks ready?" Bailey picked up a tray at the counter Robert was now working behind.

The door chimed behind her. Robert nodded his head in greeting to whoever had come in.

"Selena gets the espresso, straight up." He loaded Bailey's tray. "And Margo likes her lattes."

"Selena?"

"The artist."

Ah.

The woman wearing the vibrant combination of a deep plum tunic and sage-green skirt, who Bailey could have sworn she'd met somewhere before.

"You came!" She heard Selena exclaim.

Bailey turned. Her experienced hold on the tray of steaming drinks deserted her at the sight of Derrick Cavenaugh holding the beautiful artist's hand and smiling as he chuckled—genuinely chuckled—at something she was saying.

Crash!

Then everyone was staring at Bailey and the broken pottery littering the floor.

BAILEY GREENWOOD...

Derrick had wrangled her name out of her boss, while he'd failed once again to talk the irritated man into dropping the shoplifting charges.

Little Bailey Greenwood...

The name was vaguely familiar, but besides the heather-green eyes, he had only a distant memory of an overly bright kid who, as a freshman, had kicked his and everyone else's butts in senior calculus class.

And now she was working the counter at a suburban minimart?

The kid behind the Stop Right register hadn't blinked before spilling that his coworker wasn't on her way home at six in the evening.

Bailey's always scrambling for work. I think she's hooked up with some coffee place in SOMA, something like two nights a week....

Leslie had shot into her room and locked the door after their silent drive home. The sitter was already paid for, since Derrick had planned to stay at the office late to work on Reynolds-Allied briefs. He'd made sure Savannah was settled, then he'd headed back to town, to track Bailey down. Maybe to talk her into...

Into what?

After he'd treated her like a nobody back in Langston, he had no right to ask for anything.

"Oh, dear." One of the women sitting with Selena set off to help Bailey clean up.

"I'm sure babes swoon at your feet on a daily basis," teased Selena, his only friend from high school who'd never been impressed by his impending greatness. The only Western alumni he'd kept up with over the years. "But I bet having one throw food is a new twist."

"Yeah, well, I wasn't at my charming best when we met a little while ago." Derrick winced. "I didn't expect her to be excited to see me again, but—"

"Wait. You followed Bailey Greenwood here?" Selena glanced at her remaining friend. "I should have known it would take a woman to get him to come."

"Come where?" He was only half listening.

Bailey had hustled the dripping tray into what looked like the kitchen. He glanced at the clock on the wall. He had a preteen at home on crime watch.

"Derrick, this is my friend Nora Clark," Selena said. "She's one of the parents I've been telling you about. You know, the group that might be able to help you work things out with Leslie and Savannah."

Group?

Derrick groaned.

He'd stumbled into the middle of the single-mother gabfest Selena had been pimping for the last few months. Panic didn't begin to describe the sudden urge to make himself scarce.

Selena was a successful installation artist. She had her own kid to keep track of. Where did she find the time for a sorority-esque coffee klatch?

"If you'll excuse me." He left as the woman he'd heard someone call Margo headed back their way.

Pushing through the swinging door Bailey disappeared behind, he found a brightly lit industrial kitchen that looked like it turned out a lot more than the simple desserts offered at other San Francisco coffee houses. The sound of running water led him around a corner.

"Employees only back here, buddy," the dynamo

scouring the tray said without glancing up from the sink. "Health department regulations."

Bailey looked even more exhausted than she had back at the store. Embarrassed, too, which had clearly upped her determination to avoid him.

"I'm sorry." He held up his hands. "I had no right to jump down your throat earlier. My only excuse is that it was my first stint picking my child up at a crime scene, and I was too worried about Leslie to thank you for your help. Someone mentioned you might be here tonight. I came to apologize."

"But I thought you and Selena…" She wiped at the wisps of hair that had curled free of her ponytail, then dove back into scrubbing, even though the last of the coffee had already swirled down the drain. "Never mind. If you're so worried about your daughter, shouldn't you be home, sharing your concern with your family, instead of me?"

"Well, I also wanted to…"

He was talking to the top of her head.

"Bailey—" He reached over her shoulder and turned off the tap.

"Hey!" She spun around to push him away with soapy hands. Moisture seeped through his shirt. "Back off."

She was barely tall enough to reach his chest. The soft, brown hair she wore in a ponytail smelled like cinnamon.

Taking several steps back, he cleared his throat.

"I wanted to ask if you'd consider helping my daughter just a little more," he forced himself to say. "Leslie's a good kid who's confused and trying to deal with everything that's changed in her life over the last couple of years. She needs time. She needs a chance to start over, but your boss is determined to make an example of her. If you could help change his mind, you'd be making a huge difference in a young girl's life."

Bailey's eyes drained of the promise to slap him if he invaded her personal space again. The spunk she'd been running on seemed to fizzle, along with the soap bubbles oozing down the sides of the sink.

"I had a few minutes back at the Stop Right." She wiped her hands on her apron. Smoothed them over the tendrils of hair framing her delicate cheekbones. "Beyond that, I'm fresh out of time to make a difference in anyone's life."

The hitch in her voice, the tears in her eyes as she brushed by, was a new low Derrick hadn't thought his day could sink to. He had somehow hurt her. And that was dirty pool.

If Bailey were still just pissed, that would be one thing. Having to ask a near stranger for help wasn't his strong suit, but if she'd fired off another put-down, flashed another of those scathing looks, called him an inept father, he would have followed her back into the bistro and tried to reason with her some more.

But causing Bailey Greenwood even more distress tonight was out of the question, no matter how desperate he was.

CHAPTER THREE

LESLIE SNUCK OUT of her bedroom window, leaving the house and her Saturday morning babysitter behind, and headed across Langston to meet up with Julia Parker. Her dad would be working in the city all day—*again*. And their stupid neighbor had fallen asleep on the couch, while Savannah zoned out on cartoons.

Bolting from house arrest had been so easy, it was embarrassing.

You're a smart girl, her dad had insisted last night. *Smarter than this. We'll figure out a way to get the shop owner to see reason. But you've got to stop trying to get back at me by trashing your life.*

She hated him.

She hated her mom.

Her stupid life.

The stupid box of condoms she'd been caught stealing.

Ginger Nash had called her a baby, because Leslie had never even seen a rubber. So just to prove how *grown up* she was, what had Leslie done? She'd chickened out of buying them and tried to grab-and-go instead.

Still, she'd gotten what she wanted. The news of her crime had spread all over Langston. It had even made it as far as her little sister's elementary school by yesterday afternoon.

Are you going to jail? Savannah had asked over frozen dinners and Kool-Aid last night.

Of course she's not going to jail!

Their dad's fist had pounded the table beside his plate of microwaved-beyond-recognition lasagna. He'd promised to fix the mess Leslie had made, then he'd squeezed Savannah's hand, because she'd started to cry. He might be the *Mighty DC,* but tears got to him every time. They'd gotten Savannah an extra story before bedtime.

Well, Leslie didn't want another story. She didn't want her dad to fix things here. She wanted her life in Atlanta back. Things the way they used to be. She wanted her dad to have the guts to admit that their West Coast new start sucked.

Why did he have to look like he was going to puke every time she talked about going home? Sure, her mom was in Atlanta, parading around with her new husband like she was all that. But if both her parents were going to ignore Leslie, at least they could let her have her friends and her old school back.

Crossing the street to get to the bookstore Julia had said to meet at, Leslie scrubbed at her eyes.

Wiping away tears was different than crying.

"You ready to go?" Julia asked around the straw in her can of Coke. "Ginger's mom's gone for the weekend, and her grandmother's book club is meeting until five. No one will bother us as long as we stay in her basement."

Mrs. Nash was always gone, and Ginger knew how to make the most of every opportunity to make trouble. And a little more trouble was exactly what Leslie needed.

"Let's go." She grabbed at Julia's Coke and took a swig that didn't quite settle her stomach. She'd be grounded for the rest of her life after this.

Whatever.

As long as it got her dad out of his fancy downtown office and back on this side of the bay. Then maybe he'd see that Leslie didn't fit here, and he'd take her and her sister back to Atlanta.

Their family's move to a new city on a new coast wasn't going to work.

Leslie planned to make sure of it.

"WE OWE TEN THOUSAND DOLLARS in back taxes." Beverly Greenwood gulped at her granddaughter's double take. "Travis thinks he might have missed a few things on a couple of our returns."

"What was his first clue?" Bailey dropped the IRS audit summons to the kitchen table.

Why had Beverly thought it was a good idea to have their addled, retired CPA neighbor do their taxes for free?

Because it was free!

For a word that basically meant nothing, *free* could be terribly important to a woman in Beverly's financial bind. And the inn's balance sheet had been chafing for years.

Seven o'clock on a Sunday morning was too early for dire business strategizing, but their weekend guests, including newlyweds, would be expecting breakfast soon. Four of the inn's six suites were booked. A nice ratio for the fall season, and Beverly should be grateful for the business. Still, there'd be three loads of sheets and towels to do. Four, once the linens from the dining room were cleared. All before she started on the light lunch the inn now included in the room rate.

The day-to-day grind of keeping the family business afloat was fast becoming an exercise in futility.

There'd been little time for anything but survival the last couple of years. She and Bailey were exhausted. Bookings were down. Their inn didn't have the high-end trappings vacation travelers looked for these days. Or the "location, location, location" on the San Francisco side of the bridge, that would have smoothed over the quainter parts of their establishment.

Beverly didn't mind covering the housework, now that they'd cut their staff to the bone. Or cooking most of the day, since they could no longer afford to bring in even the simplest dishes from local vendors. This place was the only home, the only life, she'd ever known.

But her granddaughter, her beautiful, brilliant granddaughter...

Bailey had been running the business side of the inn since her father died. Not to mention scrambling for whatever money she could make elsewhere. She'd given up so much, taking more on her strong shoulders than should ever have been hers. Putting her own dreams on hold year after year.

"I should have double-checked Travis's returns." Bailey dropped her head into her hands.

"You've been a little busy lately, keeping our buns out of the bank's fire."

"Yeah, well, the government wants its crack at our buns now." Bailey had meant to reassure her grandmother, but her pun fell flat. "We don't have ten thousand dollars, Grams."

The panic that came with the realization was nothing new. Bailey had once collected labels like *promising* and *gifted.* Her grandmother, her *dad,* had been so proud. They'd given her every chance to stretch her wings and fly into the future they'd assured her was within her grasp.

Then in a blink, that future was gone.

Her father's fatal heart attack at forty-five had been explained away by a genetic defect. No one could have known anything was wrong. It hadn't been anyone's fault, the doctor kept saying. As if assigning blame was the point.

Bailey had lost her world. The center of everything that her life had revolved around.

Almost everything.

She hadn't lost Grams. And they hadn't lost the inn yet. Saving this place had gotten her and her grandmother through the darkest of the last eleven years.

"We can meet with the auditor, right?" There had to be a way to make this work. "We'll explain our situation and figure something out."

"Honey…" Her grandmother's sigh reeked of giving up. "There's just so much we can do. I didn't mention it before, but a lawyer called a few months ago. He has a client looking to expand their spa franchise to the West Coast. Maybe we should—"

"No!"

Their family had scraped and fought through the Depression. After Grandpop died in World War Two and left Beverly to raise an infant son alone, Grams had somehow made it by. Then Bailey's dad had slaved to turn the aging historical building into a thriving bed-and-breakfast, not once thinking of bailing, not even when Bailey's mom had lost her battle with ovarian cancer when Bailey was still a baby. He'd taken care of what he'd had left—his mother and Bailey, and this house.

At eighteen and on her way to Yale on a full scholarship, Bailey had had bigger dreams to follow than picking up where he'd left off, but she'd stayed in Langston. Making sure Grams and this place kept going had become Bailey's new dream.

"I'll just work harder." Hard work didn't scare her. Giving up did. "Let me take a look at the returns. Maybe we have room to finagle the numbers, or work out a payment schedule with the IRS."

"Our bills are already eating us alive," Grams reasoned.

"There are better part-time jobs than the Stop Right. There's always a demand for temp work, especially at night."

"Oh, no you don't. You almost killed yourself trying to keep up with that kind of schedule last time. You can't work all night long, after putting in full days here."

"It would only be for a while."

"Ten thousand dollars isn't a while. How much longer do you expect me to let you put your life on hold—"

"As long as it takes." They weren't selling their home to some megaconglomerate that would strip the floors and high-end upgrade everything in sight.

Bailey refused to give up, no matter how easy an out Grams was trying to give her. "Maybe I can get a raise out of Drayton. I've been doing his books on the side for over a year now. He needs me. He can either make me a salaried manager, or I walk and find something else."

"Excuse me," a rough voice intruded.

The man standing in the kitchen's doorway looked even rougher.

"There was no one at the reception desk, and I heard voices back here." Derrick Cavenaugh didn't do embarrassed well. He gifted Grams with an apologetic smile. "I know it's early. I'm sorry to intrude, but I need to speak with Bailey, if she has a few minutes."

He wore threadbare jeans and sneakers with the same effortless sophistication as the other day's business suit. His white pullover spotlighted a chest just as drool-worthy as ever, sprinkled at the open neck with dark hair to match the unruly waves on his head. The beginnings of a scruffy beard had Bailey daydreaming about sexy beach strolls at dawn. Warm summer evenings spent on the inn's wraparound porch, drinking wine and watching seagulls coast overhead on the wind that curled up from the bay…

She headed to their industrial-grade coffeemaker. Being blindsided by the inn's latest financial black hole, Bailey could handle. Being stalked by Derrick

Cavenaugh twice in one lifetime called for a fresh infusion of caffeine.

"Grams, you remember Derrick, don't you?" she asked as she tripped over the frayed cuffs of her own jeans. The denim practically covered her toes.

Dressed to scrub bathrooms, not receive company, she'd grabbed the first thing she found in her closet. Not that today's couture was much different than any other day's. Just older. Not that she normally cared.

But nothing about how she felt around Derrick had ever been normal.

"Of course I remember Mr. Cavenaugh," Grams gushed. "Everyone in the area followed the excitement of your college career. How you went on to work for one of the top law firms in Atlanta. It was big news, you moving back to the San Francisco area after making such a success of yourself."

SUCCESS? Derrick mocked silently as he returned Mrs. Greenwood's friendly smile.

He'd washed out of the career he'd been molded for from birth, and his father hadn't been able to look at him the same way since. He'd chosen corporate law as his second career, because the high-profile work and the social schmoozing required to retain top-shelf clients were a playing field where he knew he could excel. And success was what he'd let himself believe he'd made, right up until his wife started screwing around with his best friend. Now he was divorced, starting over again, he'd lost complete control of his oldest daughter and he was living on borrowed time with his youngest.

"It's about Leslie," he said to Bailey. "If it wasn't important, I wouldn't be bothering you again. If you could just give me a few minutes."

He'd done his research before coming over. Because of Selena's relationship with the bistro owner and her contacts around the Langston community, Selena had been able to fill him in on Bailey's battle to keep her and her grandmother's business going. He shouldn't be here, asking for an enormous favor. But he had to reach his daughter before it was too late, and Bailey's help could be too important a factor not to try one more time. Without her, he had no chance of reasoning with the Stop Right's crotchety owner.

"All right." Bailey cast a sideways glance toward her grandmother.

The attractive older woman turned to the double range set into the wall and opened the top oven door to check on the pastry inside. Derrick's mouth watered. His empty stomach screamed.

He'd grabbed a bagel on the way to the office yesterday. Then everything since the call from Ginger Nash's grandmother was a blur. He doubted he'd even eaten, though he vaguely remembered heating a frozen pizza for the girls.

"Coffee?" Bailey motioned toward the cabinet filled with mugs.

"Sure, thanks."

Handing him the steaming mug, Bailey motioned toward the dining room that opened off the kitchen. He stopped short of begging for some of whatever marvelous creation was baking in the oven. When they sat and Mrs. Greenwood appeared, laying a plate of sugary pastry beside each of them, Derrick nearly kissed her hand.

"You two take all the time you need," she said after waving away his thank-you. "Our guests don't usually make an appearance before nine on Sunday."

Derrick peeled away a layer of cinnamon, butter and crisply baked dough, then began tearing it into bits. He couldn't swallow if he tried. Couldn't look Bailey in the eye. These were good, hardworking people who didn't need to worry themselves with his problems.

Bailey's level gaze said she was thinking pretty much the same thing.

"There's nothing I can do to get your daughter out of whatever Drayton's decided to do," she said on a sigh. "I wish there was."

There was no residue of Thursday's hostility in her tone. Only heartfelt concern for a child she barely knew.

And that compassion gave Derrick the upper hand.

He shook his head at the smug thought. Lawyers

were manipulative bastards, and he'd worked hard to become one of the best.

"I'm not trying to get her out of it anymore. I want to offer Drayton a deal, but the man's not returning my calls."

"What kind of deal?"

"My daughter was caught smoking pot with her friends yesterday morning. Whatever phase Leslie's going through, her behavior's spiraling more and more out of control, and nothing I've tried so far has made a dent. Help me convince your boss to put her butt to work. No salary. The length of time is up to him. I'll agree to whatever he thinks is equitable, to work off her crime. Leslie has to start facing the consequences of what she's doing, before I lose her for good."

CHAPTER FOUR

A LARGER-THAN-LIFE champion becoming a desperate single parent wasn't an easily stomached sight, certainly not before breakfast.

Bailey didn't know which made her sicker, Derrick's heartbreaking concern for his child, or the thought of how Drayton would take advantage of it.

"You and your wife might want to reconsider—"

"My *ex*-wife's back in Atlanta with her new husband, sweating the real-estate market, because the two-point-five-million-dollar palace he bought five years ago is in Windward. Seems Buckhead would be better for Amanda. She doesn't want to have to drive the Ferrari too far when she's ready to shop. With all those details on her mind, Leslie's commitment to ruining her life seemed like a preteen phase the last time we spoke."

Bailey blinked as Derrick pulverized the last of his cinnamon roll, adding *bitter* and *divorced* to her growing list of things she hadn't expected in this grown-up version of her schoolgirl crush.

"I'm really sorry, Derrick." She shook her head at the memory of the stunning blonde she'd heard he'd married, the cheerleading captain who'd ruled Western at Derrick's side during Bailey's freshman year. "I hadn't heard about the divorce. I've been a little out of touch the last few years."

A tired, defeated man looked up from his plate, instead of the conquering hero he played so well for the rest of the world.

"I don't remember much about you back in school," he admitted. "Except you laughing once, when you passed Amanda and me in the hall. Something about hoping I liked hanging out with leeches, 'cause I'd be paying for the privilege for as long as Amanda held on. Looks like you were right."

"And you're still paying." Bailey winced. Had she really been that much of a snot?

"No, my kids are paying, and I haven't protected them any better than I did myself. Alimony and child support were Amanda's priorities during the divorce. To get the settlement she wanted, she asked for joint custody of the girls. But ever since she married her NFL superstar, Leslie and Savannah have been with me, and Amanda's showing no sign of wanting them back."

"Kids could definitely cramp a socialite's style." Or a successful lawyer's. "So you brought them cross-country and away from the rest of your family. Why?"

"My parents are retired to Florida now. Leslie and

Savannah have only met Amanda's mother a couple
of times. And Langston was someplace new. A slower
pace than living in downtown Atlanta. And the job
with my new firm promised a partnership as soon as
I close the deal I've been working on since I got here."

"Nice." Something too much like envy tainted
Bailey's response.

"Yeah, except I'm no better at being a single father
here than I was at being a married one in Atlanta.
That's why I came over to—"

"I can't help you, Derrick." She couldn't even get
through the morning without needing a contingency
plan for outmaneuvering the IRS.

"You could reason with your boss. Pull a few
strings. Get Drayton to see that putting Leslie to
work would be a win-win proposition for the store.
What does he have to gain by taking her to court?"

Derrick had been close to pleading when he
arrived. Now, annoyance glittered behind the slate-
gray eyes he shared with his daughter.

The man was a champion. He'd probably never
had to beg for anything. He'd never scraped by on
nothing, not even pride.

"By all means, see what you can talk Drayton in
to, but count me out," Bailey said, not liking herself
much while she said it. "My boss is a hard-ass, and
whatever markers I hold at the store, I need them to
work out my own Hail Mary deal."

"You really care that little about what happens to a messed-up twelve-year-old?"

Ah-ha. The gloves were off, and that made things easier all around.

"You know, you didn't even know I existed before Thursday." She picked up her plate and mug as she stood. "How is it that you've got my self-centered motives all figured out, in just a matter of days?"

Derrick was standing, too, lending height and muscle to the devastating good looks that had turned her to goo as a teen.

"Bailey—"

She raised her free hand to stop him.

"I may have had a crush on you, along with every other girl at Western, but you were full of yourself then, and you're full of yourself now. I get that it sucks that the world's not revolving around you anymore, and that you've got more to deal with than your fancy new career. But my advice is to stop feeling sorry for yourself. You always were smarter than any of your crowd gave you credit for. Find a way to solve your own problems."

"Feeling sorry for myself? Is that what you call being willing to beg a stranger for help, no matter how pointless it obviously is?"

"No, it's what I call being so wrapped up in your own world that you can't see the mess crashing down on other people!" With his degree and experience, not to mention his high-profile image, he could write his own ticket in whatever city he chose to live in. But *she* was selfish, for not sticking her neck out to spare him the embarrassment of crawling back to Drayton? "I have my own problems, Derrick. I get that you don't care what they are, but they're just as real to me as Leslie's are to you."

"I…" He jammed his hands in his jeans' pockets. "I'm sorry, Bailey. I shouldn't be pushing like this. I heard what you've been doing since high school. And I can only imagine how hard it must be to keep this business going for your grandmother. You must be busy as hell, but—"

"Busy! I'm not *busy,* and I'm not putting you off because I think my problems are more important than yours. I'm drowning, Derrick…."

A hiccuping sound escaped her attempt to swallow. She never let the past in. With today and tomorrow to worry about, who had time? She just kept working. Kept her head down. Refused to give up.

"Bailey." He reached for her arm.

"Don't waste your pity on me." She backed toward the kitchen, clutching her dishes to keep from tossing them at his head. Something raw and ugly had been building since first seeing Derrick in all his successful glory. Resentment she'd never before felt toward anyone or anything. "Save your energy. I know it must be tough being dumped by the woman of your dreams and starting over with a new six-figure opportunity in your fabulously successful law career, saddled with two kids someone else was supposed to be taking care of. But spare me the sob story. You'll find a way to handle Leslie's problems, just like you've handled everything else in your life. When you've hit rock bottom and have no way out except letting down the people you love, then maybe we'll talk about running out of options."

He should hate her for what she was saying—she did.

But if his problems that weren't really problems didn't get out of her house, she was going to embarrass herself and burst into tears for the first time since her father's funeral. Derrick Cavenaugh made her remember a world she didn't have time to think about anymore—the one from her dreams, where she got to risk everything and win, instead of fighting the never-ending, losing battle she'd been stuck in for over a decade.

Derrick's eyes narrowed. The hand that had been reaching toward her returned to his side, his fist clenched.

"I'm sorry for intruding on your morning." He turned to go, but stopped at the door to the hall. "You know, I get that I've had my life handed to me on a silver platter. Things have been easy for so long, I'm not sure I'd know the high road if it rolled up to my house and rang the doorbell. But there's nothing more rock bottom than watching my little girl ruining her life."

Maybe it was the gruffness in his voice, or the terrified love ringing in each word, but after he left, Bailey sat back down, instead of heading off to tackle her Sunday morning chores.

She'd railed at Derrick, when it was her life that was driving her crazy. She'd judged him, because she'd never felt more like a loser herself. And she'd totally disrespected the very real threat he faced of not getting through to his daughter.

Since when had her pain-in-the-butt life become an excuse for being an unfeeling bitch?

"WHAT'S UP?" Selena asked over the phone. "You sound wrecked."

"Nothing new." Derrick rubbed at the shooting pain behind his right eye. "Leslie's gone again."

"I thought you grounded her."

"Yeah, well, that seems to mean about as much to her as everything else I say."

Bailey had accused him of feeling sorry for himself. Truth was, he was terrified.

The happy, sweet little girl he'd known was gone, and the prickly preteen who'd taken her place was determined to hurt herself and everyone around her.

"Do you know where she went?" Selena said over a commotion on her end of the line.

"What's going on over there?" he asked.

"I'm working on a mixed-media project I owe a client." A loud crash nearly drowned out her words. "Of course Drew and Axel are demolishing my studio faster than I can get anything done. So, you're going after Leslie, right?"

Bailey's fierce expression flashed through his mind. *Find a way to solve your own problems.*

"I think I know where she went." Right back to that girl Ginger's house. For no other reason than he'd forbidden her to. "Once I find her, we have some damage control to do this afternoon, at the convenience store she shoplifted at Thursday."

He was going to convince the crabby owner to see things his way, whatever it took.

"Savannah can hang out here for as long as you need," his friend offered.

"I can't ask you to do that," he forced himself to say. Selena sometimes slaved over an installation for months. Her work had been featured in some of San Francisco's premier office buildings. She didn't need another kid hanging around, adding to the confusion.

Not to mention that he should be spending his first Sunday off in months *with* Savannah, rather than pawning her off on someone else.

"You didn't ask," Selena countered. "I'm offering.

Can't promise you won't get the kid back covered in oil paint and dog slobber, so you might want to drop her off in the rattiest play clothes she's got. But it's about time you're confronting Leslie. I'll even keep Savannah overnight and get her to school in the morning, if you think it'll help."

Selena had been pressuring him to wake up for months. But he'd been too focused on clinching the Reynolds-Allied deal to listen. Then Leslie had upped the stakes.

"I could use the afternoon to work some things out," he finally said. "But—"

"Then take it. Go do the dad thing. Savannah will keep Drew and the Tasmanian Devil busy. We'll be fine here." Another crash was followed by Selena's frustrated groan. "As long as Drew *stops playing fetch in the loft!*"

The last of her statement had been screamed for her middle schooler's benefit. Derrick chuckled in spite of his lousy morning, and the even lousier afternoon to come.

Do the dad thing.

Whatever the hell that was.

CHAPTER FIVE

DOING SOMETHING DUMB for a good reason didn't make it any less of a bad idea. But dumb or not, Bailey couldn't stop herself from knocking on Larry Drayton's door.

She had a lot riding on getting a promotion and the salary increase that would come with it. But not trying to help Leslie Cavenaugh wasn't an option. Apparently, neither was forgetting the heart-stopping picture the girl's father had made as he'd left the Gables that morning.

This wasn't about doing a favor for an old crush, she reminded herself. Or about making the world better for a man whose reality was already ten times better than hers. This was a one-time shot to help give a second chance to a mixed-up kid whose life had been turned upside down.

Something Bailey understood more than she cared to.

And the sooner she got this over with, the sooner she could hit up Drayton with her own agenda.

She knocked again.

"What!" he bellowed from inside, as close to *come in* as he ever managed.

She hadn't taken two steps into the office before she tripped over her feet, coming face-to-face with her really dumb idea, multiplied by a factor of two.

Leslie Cavenaugh was slouched in the same ugly chair as before, the waist of her too-short shorts ending way below the hem of her revealing halter top. Just looking at the kid's platform sandals made Bailey's feet hurt. And beside her sat a stunned, absolutely delicious-looking Derrick.

Bailey turned to beat a path back to her car.

"Oh, no you don't!" Drayton griped. "I had a feeling you were behind this nonsense. You're not dumping this in my lap, then hightailing it out of here. I'm not letting this girl work off her crime, unless you agree to be responsible for her hours."

"Me?"

"If not, I'm pressing charges. I got no time to supervise the little thief. You either keep an eye on her, or there's no deal. I don't care how many free hours Mr. Cavenaugh says he's willing to let her work."

"Bailey's not—" Derrick was on his feet.

"I'm not—" Bailey said over him, then stopped.

Please tell my boss this isn't a good idea, she begged Derrick with her gaze.

Deciding to put in a good word for the kid was one

thing. Agreeing to supervise Leslie's time, when Bailey's schedule was already stretched to the breaking point, wasn't going to happen.

"This is my daughter's mess," Derrick argued. "Leslie needs to be the one to clean it up. There's no reason to make more work for Bailey."

"Well, the girl's sure as hell not going to hang out here after school without someone keeping an eye on her. And Bailey's the only employee I'd trust to do that."

"After school?" Bailey said through the shock of receiving the first ass-backward compliment she'd ever received from the man.

"I get to come straight here when I get off the bus." Leslie sounded as if she couldn't be more bored. "Then call my dad from the pay phone outside, because my cell phone is now contraband. Then I get to work for nothing until he swings by whenever he can manage to make it home from work."

"I'll be here at six every afternoon until we have this cleared up." Derrick had his daughter's undivided attention for the first time. "If Mr. Drayton and Ms. Greenwood agree to this, you owe them another apology and a thank-you. And you'll damn well show up where you're supposed to be every afternoon, on time and ready to work. Ditch to hang out with your friends just once, and I'll drive you down to the courthouse myself, and file the charges for Mr. Drayton."

"Like you care where I go, as long as I'm out of your way." Tears welled in Leslie's heavily made-up eyes. "So you're forced to spend time with me for a while. So what? I know you'd rather be in town kissing your boss's butt."

Bailey couldn't breathe.

She'd fork over any number of body parts to have just one more afternoon with her father. The same kind of longing had filled Leslie's outburst. Instead of a preteen gone wild, they were listening to a little girl who missed her daddy.

"I suppose I could come in a few hours each afternoon," she heard herself promising, even though she'd hoped to snag more better-paying bistro hours instead.

Derrick's relieved smile made taking her offer back impossible.

"You either work a full shift, or you'll be doing it on your own time," Drayton warned. Half shifts were a cardinal sin at the well-oiled machine that was the Stop Right. "I'm not—"

"Oh, you'll pay me, because I'll spend the time straightening out the twisted mess you make of your books every quarter, instead of working unpaid overtime on the weekends." It was uncomfortably easier to stiffen her spine and demand her due with a former college all-star standing beside her, frowning at Drayton on her behalf. "And there's the matter of the management title you'll be giving me, along with the raise I should have as *the only employee you trust*. But for now, do the right thing. Think of the good it will do your reputation in Langston. Show everyone you have a heart. Give a twelve-year-old a break."

"A chance to learn from her mistakes," Derrick added.

"Come on, Larry," she reasoned. "You don't really want this town to think you're too much of a crank to lift a finger to help a kid who's willing to pay for her mistake working for you for free."

Drayton's jaw dropped. She could see the silver fillings capping six back teeth.

She'd called him Larry.

She'd pushed back, rather than accepting his crappy attitude as part of a job she couldn't afford to lose.

Derrick planted his hands on his hips, muscles hardening beneath the soft knit of his shirt. Leslie slid closer to the edge of her chair.

"Fine." Drayton threw his arms in the air. "But I want the girl working. And if she doesn't show for a single shift, I'm calling the police back and refiling charges. You're getting off easy, little girl. Don't make me regret it."

The twelve-year-old who'd been sulking when Bailey arrived was too busy gawking at her dad to respond.

"Answer the man." Derrick's hand cupped his daughter's shoulder.

"Yes, sir." The kid leaned into her father's touch as she faced Drayton. "I'll be here."

"Your daddy says your bus lets you off at your house at three-thirty, and that you can walk here," Drayton said. "You and Bailey had better be here tomorrow by quarter 'til four."

"I'll be here at three." Bailey turned away from the united front she and Derrick and his daughter had made. "We need to discuss my future here."

Her future.

Her Grandmother's future.

The raise she'd told herself she wasn't leaving without.

The exhilaration of finally standing up to her tightwad boss wilted as she walked away from the office. She'd be lucky if she didn't lose hours now, instead of increasing them.

"Bailey!" Derrick caught up with her in the narrow hallway that led into the store. "I don't know what to say. I had no right this morning, asking you to get involved in my family's problems. But if you hadn't...if your boss hadn't listened to you, my daughter would be on her way to court in a few weeks, instead of having a second chance."

He stepped closer, until she could count the soft hair peaking above the V neck of his pullover.

Smell the soap he'd showered with that morning. Wonder how he kept in such impressive shape, when he worked in a corporate office six or seven days a week.

A finger tipped her chin up until she was looking into warm gray eyes.

Good Lord.

Those eyes.

"Thank you," he said. "For showing my daughter how people stand up and do the right thing, instead of taking whatever path of least resistance is handy."

He was talking about himself, she realized.

She should apologize for the horrible things she'd said that morning. But Derrick's finger was still caressing the sensitive skin below her chin. He was too close. And yet, not close enough.

She edged away.

"I need to get going."

"Bailey." He stopped her that time with nothing more than the concern in his voice. "I don't want working with Leslie to cause trouble for you here."

"It'll be fine." Leslie wasn't the problem. Bailey being in the same room as Derrick, and not completely losing sight of her own priorities, was the problem. "Your daughter will be here a week, maybe two. It won't take long for her to learn that this is the kind of dead-end job she'd rather die than be working at in ten years."

There was that half smile again. The one that said he didn't quite understand.

Join the club.

He reached into the back pocket of his fitted-to-perfection jeans, withdrew his wallet and from it a business card, which he handed over.

"This is my work and my cell number," he said. "If there's any trouble tomorrow afternoon…"

"I'll let you know." She hesitated, then took the card.

A zing of awareness shot up her arm from where their fingers brushed. An instant of pure sensation that felt better than anything had in a long time. Good enough to tempt her with the need for more, whatever the cost.

Dear God.

What had she gotten herself into?

"I CAN'T BELIEVE I can wear your tennis shoes." Leslie snickered. "Are your feet really that scrawny?"

The first thing Bailey had done once Leslie arrived at the Stop Right was hand over an old T-shirt to replace the tank top Leslie had worn that morning—because it irked her dad that he could see the straps of her bra beneath it. Then Bailey had shoved a ratty pair of sneakers at her.

"Cracks about how you're already as big as I am," Bailey snapped, "won't end well for you, when your dad asks if you've been working and playing well with others."

Leslie couldn't stop the giggle that followed.

Maybe working in this dump wouldn't be so mind-numbing after all.

"I didn't hear your boss say anything about having to dress frumpy to do the job," she snarked, even though the sneakers were *way* more comfortable than the strappy sandals she'd worn all day.

Who knew fitting in at school could hurt her feet so much?

"Trust me," Bailey said as she handed over the same kind of band that held her own ponytail in place. "Frumpy is preferable to 'Hey, baby, you wanna wait outside 'til I'm off work?' We get a steady stream of beer drinkers in here. You won't be selling them anything, but you'll look cute enough stocking shelves for them to notice. Better make it clear that even thinking about touching you would be illegal." Bailey pointed toward the hair band. "Pull your hair back."

Eager to cooperate and grossed out by the thought of skanky guys gawking at her—Leslie made her own ponytail.

"Is that why you dress the way you do?" she asked. "Because you don't want men to notice you?"

Bailey seemed smart enough, even cute, for a grown-up. Leslie's dad had clearly thought so.

"I dress this way—" the woman looked down at

her wrinkled shirt and raggedy jeans, as if she'd just noticed them "—because what does it matter how I look when I'm hustling from one dead-end job to another, so I can make my mortgage? That's what people do when they have no other choice." She nailed Leslie with a wicked-cold glance. "A lot of people would kill for the opportunities you're throwing away. So, listen to your dad. Figure out a way not to lose the good things he's trying to make sure you have in your life."

The guy from behind the register poked his head into the storeroom as Bailey turned toward a stack of boxes.

"Someone's out here to see the kid," he said, before heading back up front.

"Oh, my God, my dad's such a tool." Leslie made her sigh extra bratty, to cover a sneaky rush of happiness.

He'd broken away from his all-important job even earlier than he'd promised, just to check on her.

"Unpack the chips in these boxes into a cart, then restock the displays out front." Bailey patted her shoulder. "I'll deal with your dad."

And even though Leslie had only known Bailey for a few days, she had no doubt that the woman could handle just about anything.

DRESSED IN paint-splattered cargo pants and a curve-hugging tank top, the woman waiting by the register looked just as exotic as she had at Margo's. The memory of how Derrick had pulled Selena Milano into a hug, laughing in an easy, familiar way, had Bailey gritting her teeth against a ridiculous spurt of jealousy.

The man could hug whomever he wanted to. What business was it of hers, if his taste in women had progressed from flighty blondes to something more substantial? Bailey was the shop girl who'd agreed to babysit his kid, nothing more.

She held out her hand. "You're Selena, right? You didn't have to stop by. I told Derrick he could call and check in."

"I don't know if you remember it or not, but I was in Derrick's class at Western. And—" A teenager and a barking whirlwind skidded down the aisle, nearly barreling into Bailey. "Drew, I told you to play outside."

"They're okay." Drayton was long gone. He'd split as soon as Bailey made it clear she wasn't backing down on her ultimatum to be made a salaried manager, or she was out of there as soon as the Cavenaugh girl was.

She smiled down at the boy and the animal.

"Just remember, if you break it, you buy it."

Having a pet to wreak havoc on her own life was on the list of nice-to-haves Bailey never gave a second thought. The must-haves kept her busy enough.

"Outside." Selena jerked her head toward the door,

raising an eyebrow as her son inhaled to argue. "You're already in the hole for two weeks' allowance. Wanna make it three?"

Boy and dog dragged their feet and paws as they trudged outside. The door's jingle snickered at the dejected picture they made.

"What on earth am I going to do with him?" Selena asked the world in general.

"Your son?"

"Him, too." The artist smiled. "Are you in the market for an overactive canine to add a little color to your uneventful life?"

"I wish." What would uneventful feel like? "He's not your dog?"

"Looks like he is now." Selena's smile widened as Leslie pushed a shopping cart full of snacks into the store. "Hey, kiddo, how's it going?"

"Is my dad with you?" Leslie tried hard to look like she didn't really care.

"No, sorry," Selena commiserated as the twelve-year-old's shoulders slumped. "Drew and I were out this way for his baseball team's pre-season meeting. I thought we'd stop and see how things were going. Nice threads," she added with a wink.

"Yeah, they're swell." Leslie shuffled toward the half-empty rack of snacks. "Everything's just *peachy.*"

"Tell her father she's doing great," Bailey offered, still trying to place Selena in her Western

High memories. But Bailey had been four years behind Derrick's class, and all she could seem to remember was him.

"You'll probably talk to Derrick before I do," Selena said. "He only shared that Leslie would be spending afternoons here because I nagged him about it. He told me not to bother you while I was in town. That he trusted you, which was unusual enough to make sure I wouldn't pass up the chance to snoop. He's one of my closest friends, but that man doesn't trust much of anyone these days, women most of all."

"Oh, well..." Bailey caught Scott Fletcher hanging on every word. She stared him down, and he finally turned back to the sitcom blaring from the small TV Drayton kept behind the register. "I guess I should get back to the office. I have to balance the weekly accounts before heading over to Margo's later."

"How are things going at the Gables?" Selena snooped on, undeterred.

Bailey hesitated, finally deciding the best response to the out-of-the-blue question was saying nothing at all.

"I know," Selena conceded. "I sound like a hopeless busybody, but I've always loved that old place. I actually stopped in the middle of the street the first time I laid eyes on it. The Victorian architecture… The picture the house makes on the edge of that bluff overlooking the bay… It's really something. I have Langston clients who bring me out this way a few times a month, and everyone around the community admires how hard you've worked keeping the inn going for your grandmother."

"Yes, well…" Everyone? "The bank still lets us live there."

For now.

"Derrick mentioned how great it looks inside. It impressed the hell out of him, when I told him you'd stayed on after your father died, instead of heading off to college."

"Bailey, you gonna be here for a few more minutes?" Scott brushed by without waiting for an answer. "I'm going out back for a smoke."

Stunned by the idea that someone like Derrick Cavenaugh, not to mention her tiny community, was impressed enough to gossip about her paycheck-to-paycheck existence, Bailey let Scott go—when she'd made it a firm rule not to enable the teenager's determination to flirt with lung cancer. Stepping behind the register, she put several feet between her and the woman smiling at her inability to respond to the most unexpected compliment she'd ever received.

She'd blown every expectation she'd ever had for her life. She'd made such a *success* of the last eleven years, her grandmother's business was on the last of its nine lives.

"Mom?" Selena's son poked his head inside. He held the panting, drooling dog by the collar.

"We should get going," Selena said. "Say hi to Derrick for me. See you later, Les."

She waved and headed after her son.

Leslie pushed the now-empty cart to the front of the store.

"Selena seems nice." Bailey tidied the various promotional displays crowded around the register.

"I guess." Leslie drooped against the counter in a display of preteen sulking.

"So, she and your dad been friends since high school?"

"I guess." The kid studied Bailey for a minute. "They're not dating, if that's what you mean."

Bailey knocked over the carton of dollar-store-quality penlights. "What? No, I wasn't…I mean, I'm not—"

"He hasn't dated anyone since my mom screwed him over for his best friend." Leslie fiddled with a loose thread on her T-shirt's hem. "The way I figure it, my mom started stepping out right after Savannah was born. The Mighty DC never pulled his nose out of his work long enough to notice. Not until she filed for divorce."

"Looks like you've got him noticing now." Bailey

gave the kid's shoulder a friendly nudge. "But working here is nothing compared to the price you're going to pay if you don't rein in some of the acting out. You don't want to spend the rest of the year needing a 'Get Out of Jail Free' card just to leave your house."

"So what if I don't get to go anywhere? I hate this nowhere town. Things were better back in Atlanta. As soon as my dad sees that, we'll be out of here."

You had to admire how hard the girl was willing to fight for what she wanted.

"You're not giving the Bay area a chance," Bailey reasoned. "Your dad didn't live here very long when he was a kid. Maybe he's forgotten what a good time San Francisco can be."

"Or maybe he just doesn't care." The girl turned on the heels of her borrowed sneakers, and shoved the cart toward the storage room for more not-quite-fresh snacks.

Bailey checked her watch and sighed.

She'd been supervising Leslie Cavenaugh for all of half an hour, and she was already growing more attached to the kid than was wise. Not to mention that she suddenly had an itch to stop by the pound and pick up a puppy to bring home. Then there were the memories of Derrick smiling down at her, touching her, that wouldn't stop replaying in her mind.

Selena had said he'd been impressed. Leslie had

thought Bailey was interested in dating the man, assuming Derrick Cavenaugh saw her as anything more than a convenient babysitter.

Meanwhile, Bailey needed a man in her life as much as she needed a puppy.

What she *needed* was to finish the store's books, and to keep her contact with Derrick focused on his kid. He was too much of a reminder of what she'd once dreamed of having. Dreams that would only hurt her, if she let herself want them now.

CHAPTER SIX

PRAYING FOR THE OUTCOME of football games was strictly off-limits in Derrick's world. God had better things to do than care about football.

But Derrick figured asking for a miracle for his family, one that didn't involve getting himself fired from his law firm, wasn't totally over the line.

He'd skipped out of a conference call to give himself a shot at making it over the bridge in time to pick up Leslie. But he was still almost a half hour late.

So much for divine intervention.

Braking at the curb in front of the convenience store, he got out of his car and jogged through the rain. Leslie was waiting just inside, her backpack slung over her shoulder, and her "bite me" expression at full tilt.

"I got here as soon as I could, honey." He cringed against the memory of saying exactly the same thing to his ex-wife, way too many times. "I left work early, but the weather has everything backed up. I'm sorry."

"Yeah, okay. Whatever." *Whatever* was twelve-year-old speak for *up yours, Dad.*

Leslie flicked her umbrella open, as the Western High School T-shirt she was wearing registered.

"Where did you get the shirt?" he asked before she stepped out into the rain.

"Bailey." Leslie shifted her backpack higher on her shoulder. "She said I could borrow it and the shoes. She brought them from home, almost like she hadn't raced over here at the last minute because she didn't have any other choice."

Like Derrick had, she didn't bother to add before sprinting for the car.

Bailey wasn't the enemy, he reminded himself, and his daughter was only pushing his buttons. But it still stung that someone they barely knew seemed to be hitting it off with his child better than he had in years.

"Where's your boss?" he asked the kid who had his feet propped up behind the counter.

"Who?" He barely glanced away from whatever sitcom rerun was blaring at his elbow.

"Bailey Greenwood."

Nearly Twenty and No Ambition snickered.

"She's not my boss, I don't care how old she is. She—"

"Where is she?" Derrick put just enough mean into the question to get the desired effect.

The guy's feet skidded to the floor. His eyes darted

to the wide shoulders that only fit into Derrick's dress shirts because he had everything tailor-made.

"Um, back in the office, with her head in the books, last time I saw her. I don't think she's left yet."

Derrick managed a thank-you before he headed down the hall.

Please, don't let that be Leslie in six or seven years.

"Got a minute?" he asked, as he barged into the office and found Bailey sifting through receipts and entering figures into a computerized spreadsheet.

"Do I have a choice?" She kept typing away.

"Your young protégé didn't seem to mind me coming back. If he waves everyone by that easily, he's a pretty useless watchdog."

"Scott's useless at just about everything." She shut down the file she'd been working in, and then the computer. "As usual, Larry Drayton's getting what he pays for."

She was wearing a T-shirt identical to Leslie's, down to the light stains that hadn't been completely bleached away, and the frayed V-neck collar that had once been a vibrant navy blue. Only on Bailey, the faded piping accented the upper swell of breasts that made it impossible for Derrick to focus on much else.

"Leslie did great today." She pushed the keyboard back and stood, crossing her arms. Delicate muscles rippled along her forearms. "She hardly complained at all."

"Yeah?" he managed to say around the need to know if Bailey was that temptingly toned all over. "She pretty much told me off on her way out the door."

"She's…" Bailey hesitated, as if trying to talk herself out of continuing.

"Just spit it out." He threw himself into the rickety guest chair and rubbed a hand through his wet hair. "I'm not blind. I know Leslie's pissed. She has every right to be, even though she's hurting herself more than she is me."

Bailey sat, too, and folded her hands. A fuzzy image surfaced of her doing that as a kid, while she puzzled through a particularly difficult calculus problem. At fourteen, she'd already been light years smarter than a jock like him would ever be.

"Leslie's…" Compassion softened her mouth even more. It filled those green eyes when she looked up. "Your daughter's missing you terribly."

Derrick's chuckle actually burned on its way up his chest.

"She misses her life in Atlanta," he corrected.

"She misses knowing that you care about her."

"Care!" He shoved out of the chair. "Why do you think I've hauled my girls cross-country and joined a new law firm where I have to pay my dues all over again? If I didn't care, I'd have stayed in Atlanta where my business was thriving, even though Leslie and Savannah would have had to watch the mother who doesn't have time for them swan around town with her new husband."

Bailey sighed. "I don't know if I should be saying anything or not, but Leslie talked about her mom a little today."

"She talked about…" Derrick could only stare. "What did she say?"

"That she'd known Amanda was seeing someone long before the divorce. Leslie thinks she knew before you did."

"She probably did." Derrick shook his head. "I was so consumed with work, I didn't have a clue what anyone at home was up to. Even after the separation…" He found himself needing Bailey, someone, to understand what he still couldn't. "I only saw the girls on odd weekends, when I could fit it in. I always assumed they were fine. When Amanda asked me to watch them while she was on her honeymoon, it seemed like the perfect chance to make up for lost time. But two weeks turned into a month, because Amanda and Rodney decided to stay on in Europe. Rodney wasn't due to be back for the Falcons yet. Then another month went by, because it was the perfect chance for them to stop off in the Caribbean on their way home. When Amanda finally made it back to town and still hadn't asked for the girls to come home, I finally got it."

"She didn't want them anymore?" Bailey looked ready to slap something.

"She seemed relieved when I told her about my job offer here, and that I wanted to bring Leslie and Savannah with me. In her opinion, it was high time I started showing an interest in being more than a weekend father. That was nearly a year ago. Amanda's new life was more important to her than anything in our old one, and the kids would have figured that out soon enough. I hadn't been much of a father, but I knew enough to get them out of there. Savannah's adjusted okay. Even though she misses her mom, most of the nastiness goes over her head still. But Leslie doesn't miss a thing, and she's so angry with me... With all of it."

He sucked in a deep breath and realized he was losing it. Rattling on, dumping his problems on someone who had no reason to care. Saying things he couldn't even bring himself to discuss with Selena, let alone the group of single-mother friends she'd promised would understand, if he just gave them a chance.

"I'm sorry for taking so much of your time." He headed for the door. "I just wanted to say thank you again, for helping with Leslie."

"Derrick." Bailey stepped around the desk and grabbed his arm.

Compassion warmed those emerald eyes he already found unbelievably sexy. The next thing he knew, he was leaning down, his mouth lowering to hers.

He jerked away until several inches separated them, and silently cursed. What was he doing?

"Have…" Bailey dropped her hand, a blush flaming up the soft, white skin of her neck. "Have you told Leslie anything that you just told me?"

"What?" His fingers itched to trace the pulse beating at the base of her throat.

"Have you talked with Leslie about—"

"About what a bitch her mother really is? No!" Every warm thing he felt just standing beside Bailey turned to rage. "I'm the one who ignored my marriage until it fell apart. And I'm the one who's going to make sure my girls get through this, whatever I have to do. Amanda's made her choice. One day I have to believe she'll regret it and decide to do the right thing. Until then, my kids are better off not knowing any more than they have to about why I moved them to the other side of the country. I'm here for a job opportunity, period."

"Leslie's better off hating you and your work, instead of her mother?" Bailey hesitated again. "Wouldn't it be better if your daughter knew that you're fighting so hard to make this new start work because of how much you love her?"

TOUCHING DERRICK had been a mistake.

Not keeping her focus on Leslie…

An even bigger mistake.

But Bailey hadn't been able to stay behind the

desk, any more than she'd been able to hold back her last question. Fathers loving their daughters was a sacred thing to her, one that came complete with a quicksand of emotion waiting to suck her under.

And Derrick clearly loved his girls to distraction.

How was she supposed to keep her distance from that?

"You're doing a remarkable job," she finally said. "Your girls are lucky to have you. It's just a shame you're not giving Leslie a chance to know that."

Derrick's slow smile was hell on those wayward schoolgirl fantasies. Especially when he began to finger the ragged collar on one of her oldest, least feminine pieces of clothing—the Western High T-shirt she'd bought at her very first high school football game.

The first game she'd watched Derrick play.

She'd hunted for ten minutes that morning, finally finding it at the bottom of her drawer.

"I'm pretty sure my daughter's already figured out how lucky she is to have you looking out for her." He traced her collarbone before his arm dropped back to his side. "It's been over a year since I've seen her in anything that doesn't look like a reincarnation of a Madonna video. How did you manage to get her to change?"

Raising her hand to the skin tingling from his touch, Bailey shrugged.

"I explained that some of the men coming in here for their afternoon buzz would be getting an eyefull if she didn't cover up." She raised an eyebrow as her football hero actually paled. "Hasn't anyone talked with Leslie about sex? Told her what to look out for and how to protect herself?"

Especially after the condom episode last week!

"I'm sure her mom has." Derrick's face had plenty of color now. "Besides, Leslie sneaks out in one outrageous getup after another, no matter what I say. Talking about boys…men…I—"

"You don't have a choice, not if you're going to be her mother as well as her father."

His expression softened.

"Is that what your father was for you?" he asked. While the lump in her throat refused to let her answer, he fished his keys from his pocket. "Why you understand Leslie so much better than I do?"

She shook her head against the memories and the sudden need to feel Derrick's touch again.

"That's why I know how much she really loves you, underneath all that anger. I don't have any more of a clue how to communicate with kids than you do. But even I can see that your daughter's raging because of how much she needs you."

Bailey had done her own kind of raging when her dad died. Quietly, so Grams wouldn't know, but she'd never needed anything more than she'd needed her father back and the life they'd had with him.

Somewhere, shut away deep inside, a part of her would always be raging.

"I've got to get home." Derrick checked his watch, exhaustion and defeat dragging at every word. "Savannah's sitter can't stay past six, and—"

"Six!" Bailey reached over the desk for the messenger bag she used as a purse. "I'm late for Margo's again."

"I'll walk you out." He fell in step behind her, his hand at her elbow, as if it belonged there.

"Thanks," she said as they neared the front of the store.

"For what?"

She couldn't find the words at first.

But Derrick and Leslie were still fighting for their dreams. They still had their chance together. And Bailey couldn't walk away, until Derrick understood how precious an opportunity that was.

"For being the nice guy I always thought you were." Instead of the absentee father she'd too quickly labeled him. She opened the door and exited into the humid, now rain-free September afternoon. Derrick joined her, the door shutting behind them, blocking Scott's too-interested gaze. She held out her hand. "For caring so much about your daughters."

"I'm screwing everything up, and that makes me

a nice guy?" His hand lingered in hers, his thumb absently rubbing across Bailey's palm, as if he couldn't make himself let go.

"No." She took care of the letting go herself. "Because you refuse to give up, no matter how many mistakes you make. Leslie's lucky to have you. Keep trying to get through to her, and she'll figure that out."

CHAPTER SEVEN

"I'M SORRY, there's really nothing more we can do, Mrs. Greenwood." The bank vice president barely managed *interested*. He didn't come close to sounding sorry, as he shot down Beverly's hopes for extending the inn's line of credit. "Real estate in Langston just isn't appreciating as quickly as other communities around the bay. I've explained all of this to your granddaughter, each time she applied for another mortgage."

"Each time? My granddaughter's spoken with you, too?"

"Yes." The man's eyebrows raised. "Several times over the last six months. I feel for your situation, I do. I'll keep pushing my boss for a new loan, but I'm afraid there's simply not enough equity left for him to see you as a viable candidate. If you can't keep the inn in the black, your only alternative at this point is probably to sell. A lawyer friend of mine at Hastings Chase Whitney mentioned Premier Spa's interest in West Coast expansion. I told him about your inn, and—"

"Yes." Beverly's chair scraped marble as she stood. "They've been in touch. Thank you for your time."

"Mrs. Greenwood," she heard him call from behind her.

She didn't turn back.

Her family had been banking at First National for generations. Now that relationship had dwindled to her and Bailey begging for help, while some thirty-year-old she'd never met offered to sell off their home to the highest bidder.

And Bailey had been hiding how much trouble they were in for how long? Since when did the girl hide anything from her?

Beverly pushed through the double glass doors that opened into the lobby of the fancy office tower she'd had to pay a fortune to park near. Fishing in her purse for her keys and the ticket that would get her Chrysler out of the lot, she barreled into what felt like a moving wall of extremely expensive, charcoal-gray suiting.

"Excuse me, ma'am." The wall's apology came from several inches above her, and held a slight southern drawl.

"Oh, dear, I'm so sorry." She apologized, craning her neck upward. "Mr. Cavenaugh. Oh, dear!"

She'd smashed the take-out container he'd been carrying against his dress shirt. Ham on rye and what looked like extra mustard oozed down his tie.

"Mrs. Greenwood." He pulled a handkerchief

from his pocket and, ignoring his own clothes, offered it to her. "You've got my lunch all over you."

And here she'd thought she was too old for a man, no matter how young and handsome, to turn her head. Waving the square of pristine linen away, she chuckled as she picked at the lettuce and sandwich bits sticking to her blouse.

"Call me Beverly, please. And don't you worry about me, young man. I'm wash-and-wear. But from the looks of it, you've got on a whole lot of dry-clean only."

And he wore it all quite well.

Bailey hadn't said much after Derrick's visit to the inn. But the girl clearly still had a thing for the handsome ex-football player.

"Yes, ma'am. But with two kids at home, I'm already on Sparkle Cleaners' frequent washer plan." He did the best he could with the handkerchief, finally giving up on the tie. "This'll make for a great story when I get back upstairs."

"Oh, your firm's in this building?"

"Hastings Chase Whitney. We have a suite on the twentieth floor." He glanced behind her. "You do business with First National?"

"Not as much as I'd like," she grumbled, then frowned. The bank VP said he had a friend at the firm. "Do you?"

"Not yet. But I was considering moving my

accounts over. It would be convenient to have a bank branch in the same building."

As it must be convenient to have *several* accounts to be concerned with.

"They're the oldest bank in the area," she offered. "And one of the most stable."

And it seemed they were determined to stay that way. There'd be no high-risk loans for the Greenwoods flying out of First National's doors.

"If they handle the inn's business, I'll take that as a ringing endorsement."

"Yes." Her smile slipped. Her chest squeezed as acceptance settled in. "They're our bankers, for at least a while longer."

"Why just a while?"

"Because it's starting to look like what we really need is a good real estate agent. Excuse me, Mr. Cavenaugh." Wiping at the corner of her eye, she hurried away.

Weekdays at the inn were lighter than weekends. But there were still guests to cook and clean for. To make feel welcome and coddled, so hopefully they'd rebook and pass the word along to their friends.

Except hope was getting harder to hang on to.

Especially when her granddaughter hadn't been shooting straight with her for who knew how long.

Bailey was back watching things at the inn, but she'd be leaving for the Stop Right soon, to help with the Cavenaugh girl. Then she was closing at the bistro. But come morning, they were going to sit down and talk numbers.

Keeping the business going meant a lot to Beverly. But if the situation was as hopeless as the bank VP made it sound, why were she and her granddaughter killing themselves to hold on to what they couldn't keep?

Why was Bailey still sacrificing the future she'd put off living for eleven years?

"COME ON, YOU GUYS," Leslie whispered. "Bailey will be here any minute."

This was a nightmare.

An absolute nightmare.

Ginger and the latest boyfriend her mom hated, Brett, had followed Leslie to the Stop Right. Because why miss out on the chance to torture Leslie even more?

"You really are afraid of that Greenwood bitch, aren't you?" Brett grabbed a bag of chips from an open case. "Relax. That guy up front didn't take his eyes off the TV long enough to even notice we're here."

Leslie snatched the bag away from him. "This stuff is inventoried when it comes in. Hands off!"

"You said you wanted to show your dad you don't give a shit about his stupid rules." Ginger ran her finger over a dusty shelf filled with cleaning supplies, making a face before wiping her hand on the butt of Brett's jeans. Her come-on smile for her boyfriend turned to a sneer when she looked back at Leslie. "We came by to help. But if you like doing what you're told, so Daddy can settle back into his big, important job in the city and forget all about you again, then you wouldn't be interested in our plan."

"What plan?"

Leslie suddenly hated herself for asking. For wanting to be as nasty as Ginger. But she hated her life more.

"Do you want *Daddy's* attention, or not?"

Ginger had lived with her mom ever since her parents divorced. Her mom worked even more hours than Leslie's dad. Ginger's deadbeat father had never held down a job for longer than a few months. But he showed up every Tuesday, to take Ginger to lame places like the video arcade, so he could scope out the barely legal twenty-somethings that skeezed there.

Ginger knew how to make the parents she hated pay. And Leslie wanted to be just like her.

Didn't she?

"What plan?" she repeated.

"Your dad banished you to this dump to get you off his hands, right?"

"Sort of." Actually, he'd seemed really scared when he'd thought there was no chance to talk Drayton into dropping the shoplifting charges. Then embarrassingly grateful when Bailey had helped work things out.

"So, as long as you're here, he's got some clerk babysitting you for free, and he's off the hook."

"Yeah, maybe." Except that Bailey had been kinda easy to talk to. And Leslie's dad was taking off from work early every night now, to pick her up.

"So why are you working your butt off, following the rules in this place?" Brett grabbed the chips back, opened them and scooped up a handful. "You're giving him what he wants without taking anything for yourself."

"You let your dad walk all over you like that, and you really are the dork I always thought you were." Ginger ate from her boyfriend's hand—probably some bad-girl attempt to look sexy. But a runaway chip ruined the effect when it dropped down her low-cut tank top, where she had to dig it out.

"Like I care what you think about me." Leslie was suddenly glad she hadn't dressed like the other girl for a change.

"No, you only care what Daddy thinks." Brett snickered. "Loosen up. Have some fun."

"I have fun."

"Is that why you keep trailing around after us?" Ginger mocked.

"Your old man's got a life." Brett walked over to the cases of soft drinks, beer and wine stacked in the corner. "Screw him, and go get one of your own. You could have a great party with some of this stuff. No one would miss a case or two."

He squatted to read the labels on the various twelve and twenty-four packs, his attention focused on the alcohol.

"You're crazy," Leslie said. "If you think—"

"And you're all talk." Ginger knelt beside Brett. "Oh, I love the rum punch ones."

She ripped open a case of wine coolers and pulled out a bottle.

"Want one?" She twisted the cap off. "It's no big deal. I've been stealing them from my mom's stash in the fridge since I was in elementary school."

Her smirk dared Leslie to stop her. To prove that she was too hung up on the rules and worried about getting in trouble to be cool like them. And maybe she was, because the thought of Bailey walking in on them, or of her dad finding out that she'd screwed up again, was making her sick to her stomach.

So was the fear that if he did find out, he'd simply find a new way not to have to deal with her. That she'd been wasting all this time, thinking what she wanted was to go back to Atlanta, when it didn't matter where she was. 'Cause neither of her parents were ever going to pay attention to her.

"Look, she's going to cry." Brett opened his own bottle and clinked it against Ginger's, as if that had been their plan all along. "Have a drink. Loosen up. You don't know what you're missing."

"Yeah, I do." And just that quickly, she was done.

Done with too-tight, trampy clothes and shoes that hurt her feet. Done with getting back at her dad, only to hate how she was turning into one of the creeps she had to hang with to do it.

"Get out."

"Told you she was too chicken." Ginger took another swig from her bottle, at the same time that the buzzer chirped on the back door—the employee's entrance.

"That's Bailey." Leslie peeked into the hall to see the woman step into the office to drop off her things. "I'll keep her busy while the two of you beat it. And don't bother coming back here trying to make me think you give a shit about my problems. Just stay away from me."

She headed for the office, even more sick to her stomach than before.

A part of her had wanted to take one of the wine coolers. To drink it down and wash away her problems like Ginger and Brett said it would. A messed-up part of her had, for just a second, been desperate enough for their approval to do almost anything.

Just so she wouldn't feel so alone.

"Hey, kiddo," Bailey said from behind the desk. "It's great to see you."

Her smile was so convincing, Leslie actually believed her.

"Hey? Where have you been?" She sat across from the desk, her question not just a stall tactic to give Ginger and Brett time to disappear from her life forever.

Hanging with Bailey felt good. Having the woman smile again, as she started talking about something that had held her up at the inn, actually felt really good.

At least until Leslie stopped by the storeroom twenty minutes later and found several cases of wine coolers missing, along with some beer.

"I'M SORRY," Derrick called after Bailey, as she yanked open the office door and stomped out, slinging her bag over her shoulder. He'd only wanted to help, after learning about the inn's financial problems. "I didn't mean to—"

"Don't worry about it. I'm late for Margo's. See you both tomorrow afternoon."

Okay, he could have handled that better.

"What did you say!" Leslie demanded, pushing past him to grab her backpack. "After all those lectures about me not giving Bailey any trouble, you have to come in and tick her off yourself!"

"I wasn't trying to upset her." He turned the lights off as they left.

"Guess it's your God-given talent," Leslie sniped. "Man, your tie is a mess. Do I smell mustard?"

Derrick clenched his jaw against the impulse to

rant back, to focus on the disrespect rather than the underlying cause.

Your daughter's raging because of how much she needs you.... Keep trying to get through to her....

More terrified of messing things up than he'd been of anything else in his life, Derrick reached for Leslie's shoulder. When she flinched, but didn't pull away, his barely there touch grew firmer.

"I never meant to upset you and your sister. I know I've been gone a lot, and I'm not easy to talk to, even when I'm home." He forced each word out as his chest grew tighter. "Your mother and I have made a mess of things, and I know you don't think you can trust us anymore. But I'm not the enemy, honey. I'm trying to make things better for you and Savannah. You have to believe me."

For the first time in what felt like years, he didn't see anger in his daughter's eyes. But the wariness was still there, as if believing he cared might hurt more than thinking she was in this alone. When she finally slid her shoulder free of his touch, it took every speck of discipline he still possessed not to reach for her again.

Nodding, letting the peaceful moment between them do its work, he shot a worried glance after Bailey, who was long gone.

"Is Bailey okay?" Leslie asked as they left the Stop Right and got into the car.

"I'm sure she'll be fine." Wasn't everyone *fine,*

when they were in danger of losing what they'd been fighting for years to save? "She's just...working hard to help her grandmother, and I thought maybe I could make things a little easier, after everything she's doing for you."

"Guess she wasn't interested."

"Guess not." Bailey had made it sound like he was offering her charity, rather than wanting to pay her for the great job she was doing with Leslie. "She's one determined woman, that's for sure."

He caught Leslie staring at him and turned on the radio.

Leave it to his classic rock station to be blasting out a tune about a woman working hard for her money. Like he needed the reminder of how hard Bailey worked.

And instead of letting her know how much he respected all she was doing, he'd managed to insult her.

Without asking, Leslie flipped the radio to a top forty station. Her chin lifted, almost daring him to launch into their usual argument. When he took a pass, she seemed almost disappointed.

They stopped at a light a few blocks from the house, and he turned up the volume. By the time they pulled into the driveway, his fingers were keeping up with the beat on the steering wheel. He parked in the garage and thumbed the button to close the automatic door. Neither one of them moved after he turned off the ignition, and the music along with it.

They'd just spent their least tension-filled ten minutes together in months. Leslie had pushed, and instead of shoving back, he'd let her have her way. He'd listened to her music, the way he should have been listening to her all along. Reined in the need to fix the immediate problem, because listening to his child—okay, listening to her music—was more important.

She was more important.

"You know," he said, when she finally reached for the door handle, "I don't have much work to do tonight. How about we send the babysitter home, order in some pizza and pick a DVD to watch?"

The files in his overflowing briefcase could wait.

He'd stay up after the girls went to bed, or he'd find a way to make up the time tomorrow. Tonight was going to be all about doing the *dad* thing.

Leslie's jaw-dropping reaction and the total absence of one of her smart-ass comebacks shined a spotlight on how out of place his offer sounded. Each of them had a TV in their bedroom. They never sat together as a family to watch anything anymore.

Bailey had cast him pretty much the same incredulous look more than once, with those beautiful green eyes that could reach inside him and make him see what she did—that he had to keep fighting to get through to his kids, no matter how badly he'd messed up so far.

"Go find your sister and pick out a movie," he said, unhooking his safety belt and opening the door. "I'll order the pizza."

"I'M SORRY, Bailey," Margo said. "I wish I could give you more time, but I already have the evening hours covered. It's the afternoons we're trying to fill."

Bailey had waited until her shift was over to ask, because she'd known it was a long shot, and she'd hoped to avoid as many of Margo's sympathetic looks as she could. She'd already had her fill of those from Derrick.

She couldn't stop fantasizing about him, and all he felt for her in return was pity.

"I understand," she reassured her boss.

"I wish I could help more. You've fit in so well here. It feels like you've worked with us from the start, rather than just a few weeks."

"I'm sure I'll be able to pick up more time at the Stop Right. It'll be fine."

As Bailey headed for her car, a bigger part of her than she'd realized *was* fine with the thought of spending more time at the dingy old convenience store.

Derrick stopped by the store every afternoon to pick up his daughter. And as uncomfortable as that had become, it was also the best part of Bailey's day.

Right, because things had gone so well between them that afternoon.

I had no idea you were in danger of losing the inn, Derrick had said, just before he offered her a handout. He'd offered to talk, too, if she'd wanted to. And a part of her had. The reckless part she hadn't listened to in years.

She'd all but sprinted away from the man, the same way she'd fled Margo's compassionate gaze just now.

But there'd be no escaping Grams in the morning. They were going to finish the conversation they'd barely started after Grams returned from the bank that afternoon. It was time for Bailey to take responsibility for just how badly she'd screwed everything up.

CHAPTER EIGHT

THE SUN PEEKED through gauzy yellow curtains that had shaded Bailey's bedroom windows since she was a little girl.

Her white princess furniture was long gone, replaced by her father's mahogany sleigh bed and matching chest. The rock posters that had once covered the tea-rose wallpaper were now stored in the closet. But the twists of light that warmed the dawn's lingering shadows still followed the same timeless pattern.

Her pure cotton sheets were as cozy as ever, ironed until they were soft as clouds. The savory smell of breakfast wound its way up the wide, wooden staircase, to tempt her out of bed, just as it had every other morning of her life. And for the first time since the months after her father's funeral, Bailey longed to bury her head beneath the feather pillows and hide.

The familiar wasn't her friend that morning. Her stomach rolled at the thought of heading downstairs for the bacon and eggs she was usually starving for. The inn was the home of her childhood, and keeping it had become her dream. She had fought to hold on to this place for herself, as much as for Grams. And she wasn't ready to let it go.

Shoving the bedding aside with a growl, she stomped into her bathroom to splash water on her face. Who'd said anything about letting go?

She went downstairs, dressed in jeans and another Western High shirt like the one Derrick had touched yesterday, and breezed into the kitchen, full steam ahead.

Grams was at the stove.

"Derrick popped into the Stop Right's office for a chat yesterday," Bailey announced, the skin at her neck tingling from the memory of his touch. "You forgot to mention that you'd trashed the man's suit while you were filling him in on our financial dilemma."

Grams chuckled.

"He was such a dear about the whole thing." She set a plate of scrambled eggs and bacon in front of Bailey. "He seemed more worried about my old blouse than his beautiful business clothes. That kind of consideration is hard to come by these days."

"Yes." Bailey sat and picked up her fork, then put it back down. "It was particularly considerate of him to offer to donate to our little charity, because I'm spending a few hours a day with Leslie."

"I didn't mean to say anything to him about the inn." Grams grimaced. "But it had been such a disappointing meeting, and it just came out. He's a very easy man to talk to."

"Not according to his daughter." Bailey picked at her eggs.

"Well, the girl's talking to you." Grams smiled. "Is it so terrible that her father's grateful and wants to help you in return?"

"Offering to pay me was pity, not gratitude."

And for a crazy moment, Bailey had stared at the strong, ex-quarterback shoulders filling the office doorway, and let herself believe he was there for…

For what!

If there's anything I can do to help…

He felt obligated, nothing more.

"We were in financial trouble long before the tax foul-up, weren't we?" her grandmother asked, in the same way she'd once wanted to know why her favorite chenille bathrobe had been sacrificed to make a spring wardrobe for Bailey's favorite doll.

Bailey pushed her plate away.

"Define trouble."

"According to the bank VP, you've applied for a loan more than once this year," said the shrewd businesswoman who'd worked alongside her son to create the business that was now floundering. This wasn't the Grams who'd grown content to bake and clean all day, and leave the details to her supersmart granddaughter. "Considering how long we've been paying on the second mortgage you financed five years ago, I was a little shocked to discover that we don't have enough equity to have the place painted, let alone extend our line of credit. We *have* been making the mortgage, haven't we?"

"We've been a little late a few times, but we've never missed a payment." Bailey let *a little late* sink in for a few seconds. "Income hasn't kept up with our expenses for the last year or two. A lot of our long-distance regulars are feeling the pinch of the slow economy, and they're not traveling as much anymore. Advertising the way we'd need to to reach new guests is beyond our budget. We've let go all of our staff but the gardener, and since you and I kill every green thing we touch, Mr. Chin is kind of a must-have. I was counting on the second job at the bistro to help make ends meet until recreational travel hits an upswing, but that was before the IRS came calling. I didn't want you to find out this way. I never thought you'd go to the bank yourself."

"What choice did I have? I'm not blind. I've seen how close you are to burning out." Her grandmother sounded disgusted. "I thought you were being overly cautious, not wanting to dip into our equity. So I decided to set it up and surprise you. I was going to come by the Stop Right the first night the refinance was finalized, and tell you to quit that awful place."

"I'm sorry, Grams. I was so sure we could make this work. I still am. Don't give up yet. I know I've failed so far, but—"

"Failed!" Grams rarely got angry, but when she did, her hazel eyes lit up like tiny diamonds. "Don't you dare do that to yourself. I won't hear of it. Look at this place. Maybe we're too far from the city to be on the beaten path for San Francisco's newest generation of tourists. And maybe the economy's going to decide it's time I retire, before I'm ready to. But you're the only reason we've made it this far. Look at these." She passed over a shoebox Bailey hadn't seen at her elbow. "They're just from the last two years. I have more."

Bailey sifted through the letters inside. There were return addresses from all over the country, and several international ones.

"You always handle the business mail and leave the rest for me," Grams continued. "These trickle in one and two a week. Full of smiles and thank-yous from the people who've had a lovely time staying in our home. People we haven't just served, but friends who've shared a part of their lives with us, who thought enough of our hospitality to take the time to let us know. You have no idea how much that means to me, Bailey. How happy my life has been, working here with you. Don't you dare mess that up by calling what we've done a failure. Or thinking I can't deal with the way things have turned out."

Bailey fingered the notes Grams had cherished enough to keep, and let the truth sink in. This place was so much more than a business to them both, and Bailey had let it all slip away.

"We're maxed out with most of our creditors," she admitted. A single tear rolled loose. She wiped it away. "I've gotten pretty good at negotiating more favorable terms, but sooner or later the well's going to run dry, even for me."

"I don't know. Sounds like you're a pretty dangerous negotiator to me. You've got that tightwad Drayton jumping through hoops at the convenience store." Her grandmother's eyes weren't exactly dry.

"One of these days, he might finally cough up the cash for a licensed CPA to do his books, just for the pleasure of firing me."

"You practically run that store. Look at how you've worked things out for the Cavenaugh girl. And the sweet deal you found at that bistro in the city. Employers know a good thing when they see it, and they jump all over the chance to take advantage of it."

"Except Margo's only got a few nights a week for me. Which leaves us right where we started. With my Stop Right job not being enough to cover the back taxes, even after the raise. I'm fresh out of people dying to take advantage of me."

"Hallelujah!"

"You don't mean that. We can't quit now."

"Who's quitting? I'm just tired of seeing you give up your dreams for a life somewhere else, because you think I can't get by without you here. I love what we do. The inn's meant a lot to a great deal of people, and I'll hate to see it go. But you're entirely too hung up on this idea of protecting me. Maybe I needed that right after your father died, but not now."

"But what will you do without—"

"The mountain of work around this place?" Grams asked. "I don't know, but it might be fun to find out. Sooner or later, everything ends, honey, no matter how we fight it." She stood and stepped around the table to hug Bailey from behind. "But then something amazing happens. You get to move on to the wonderful things waiting for you next. When I think of your plans for college and a career, of everything your father dreamed for you… It makes me excited to see how far you'll go, once you're free of this place."

She made moving on sound like an adventure.

Except figuring out what would come next suddenly terrified Bailey more than losing the inn. And her grandmother seemed to know it, as she hugged her even tighter.

Bailey held on to the most extraordinary woman she'd ever known, and tried to believe. Beverly Greenwood had been every heroine in every book Bailey had read. She'd been the mother Bailey had never gotten to know. And she was suddenly the strength Bailey needed to lean against, as reality closed in.

Where would *she* go next? What kind of success could she really have, after messing up everything so badly here?

A shuffling sound from the doorway startled them both. They turned in time to catch a tempting view of Derrick's backside as he headed back toward the front of the house.

"Mr. Cavenaugh?" Grams stepped toward the door and waited as Derrick retraced his steps. "My word, we find you lurking outside the kitchen often enough, I'm going to start setting another place for breakfast."

"I used the buzzer at the front desk." His concerned gaze shot warmth through limbs Bailey hadn't realized were ice cold.

"We were too wrapped up in ourselves to hear." Grams nudged Derrick into the kitchen and toward Bailey. "That's why we unlock the door once we're up in the morning. Our guests have free run of the grounds. A lot of them like to sit on the porch and watch the sun come up over the bay. And you never know who'll be popping in from the neighborhood."

Her not-so-subtle mission to get Derrick to sit beside Bailey accomplished, Grams edged back toward the door. "I have some bushes outside that need watering."

"I didn't mean to interrupt." Derrick braced his elbows on the table. "But—"

"But it was just too tempting to pass up, right?" Bailey felt a bout of bitchiness coming on, and she gave in to it. Why did Derrick Cavenaugh, of all people, have to be there to witness her rock bottom? "For an ex-jock still having trouble adjusting to the real world, it must be exhilarating to get a play-by-play of how badly someone else is messing up for a change."

He pressed a finger to her lips, and all she could do was stare at the way his chest filled out his expensive dress shirt, and absorb the incredible sensations radiating from his touch.

"But," he continued, "I'm glad I did. I already knew how hard you were working to keep this place going. But until now, I didn't really get what that meant. I'd give anything for someone to look at me the way your grandmother looks at you."

His finger slipped away as his eyes dropped to Bailey's lips.

She had absolutely no idea what he was talking about. Still couldn't imagine why he was there, barging into her home, her life—again. All she knew was that she wanted, needed, his touch back.

DERRICK'S HEAD lowered toward Bailey, even though he was certain it was a bad idea. Even though he should already be out the door.

He'd never wanted anything more than the kiss he'd been denying himself for days. Each time he'd seen her, he'd found a reason to touch her. And each time had left him wanting more.

Now, he couldn't stand not knowing what someone so genuinely unselfish tasted like.

He'd been considered a champion most of his life. A winner since playing rec ball in elementary school. To many, *a hero.* But none of the accolades could compete with the admiration Beverly Greenwood so clearly felt for her granddaughter.

"Derrick?" Bailey's perfect pink lips trembled as he sunk his hands into the curls she hadn't smoothed into a ponytail that morning.

"Let me," he whispered, drowning in her shocked eyes, begging with his own. "Bailey, please. Let me…"

He'd stopped by on the way to work to apologize for yesterday's verbal clumsiness, and to make sure it hadn't changed Bailey's mind about helping his daughter. At least that's what he'd told himself, when he'd decided he could afford to be late getting to the office, even though he had to take off early to pick Leslie up that afternoon.

Truth was, *this* was what he'd come for.

He needed to be one hundred percent focused on Reynolds-Allied today, and on Leslie and Savannah when he got home. But as Bailey's lips met his, seeking instead of waiting, needing instead of merely accepting him, trembling still as they parted for his tongue and took him into her body, there was no way in hell he could stop.

He cupped the back of her head, angling her mouth for a deeper possession. This is what he'd come for. What he'd wanted from almost the moment he'd set eyes on the woman.

Bailey moaned and leaned even closer.

Her strong fingers pressed into his arms, tracing every clenched muscle as they moved upward, until her arms wrapped around his neck. His own hands went traveling in the opposite direction, down the curve of her spine until they reached the softer flesh beyond and lifted her into his lap.

Lord, he was a butt man, and Bailey Greenwood's bottom—

"Derrick?" she murmured again.

He managed a grunt as he cupped her closer, settling her legs on either side of his hips before diving back in for more of her kiss.

She pulled away. "What... What are we doing?" Her voice was still dazed, but the practical, always-thinking Bailey was reemerging from the hot, needy woman plastered against him. "It's...it's the crack of dawn. What—"

"Can you tell me a better way to greet the day." He forced himself to let go. Pecked a more chaste kiss on her nose before she scooted back to her own chair. "If your grandmother's offering a place at the table every morning…"

"Don't be ridiculous." Bailey ran a hand down her clothes in that self-conscious way he was starting to hate. "I'm—"

"Amazing." Smart and funny. Willing to help anyone. A natural leader. Gorgeous from her wrinkled, cotton shirt down to her bare feet.

"Yeah, I'm a real phenomenon." Defeat rang in every word. "What are you doing here, Derrick?"

"Crowding you." He stood and walked several feet away, creating the space they both needed.

"Stalking, you mean."

"I can't seem to help myself anymore."

"Derrick." Bailey stood, too. Cleared her throat. Didn't quite look him in the eye. "About yesterday…"

"I know. I sounded like a patronizing ass when I offered to help. But you've already made an impact on Leslie, in just a few days. Look at how much better she's dressing. How hard she's working at the store. We actually talked on the drive home yesterday. Well, *I* talked. But Leslie sat there and at least pretended to listen. We spent an evening watching a movie as a family."

The beauty of Bailey's smile drew him closer. "That's great. More time with you is the best thing you can give your girls."

"I think the best thing I've given Leslie so far is

more time with you. You understand people, Bailey, in a way I've never tried to. You make them feel important. Leslie hasn't gotten enough of that in a long time. What you're doing for her is priceless. *That's* why I offered to pay you. I should have, even before I knew how much you needed the money."

"You don't have to buy me." The last of the softness drained from her eyes. "Leslie's a great kid. Working with her feels like the one right thing I've done in a long time."

"And you think *I'm* blind!" he snapped.

He couldn't help it. A woman like Bailey constantly putting herself down was a waste. "You've built your life around helping your grandmother. You could have had the world at your feet, but you saw what was really important, and you stuck. Stop talking about yourself like you're some kind of failure. It makes you sound like a martyr, and that's beneath you."

"A martyr?" she sputtered. "Look—"

"I'd give anything to have that kind of connection with my girls." He hadn't meant to take Bailey's hand again, but he squeezed when she tried to yank away. "You've had more success, staying here in Langston, than I grabbed the whole time I was away. You have someone in your life who knows you care, who would do anything for you in return. I have an ex-wife who was never in love with me, as much as she was in love with the life she thought she could have with me. A father who has no idea how to talk to me anymore, now that football's out of the picture. And kids who've never had the quality time with either of their parents that they deserve. Leslie's already decided I'm hopeless. Savannah will figure it out soon enough. You tell me which of us is the hero in this picture."

"I…" Bailey finally pulled free. Crossed the room to fill a kettle with water and set it on a burner to boil. "I don't know what to say."

He checked his watch, then stared at his shoes. "Say you'll keep working with Leslie at the store."

"Of course."

"Say you'll spend more time with her when you can." The suggestion came from out of nowhere. But it felt right, for all of them. "I'm doing everything I can to reach her, but Leslie responds to *you*. You're a natural with her. And I'd want to pay you, to cover whatever shifts you might be missing at the bistro or the convenience store."

"Derrick." Bailey's gaze caressed his lips. As if he needed the reminder that it wasn't just for his daughter's sake that he wanted Bailey around as often as they could have her. "I don't think that's a good idea."

"I'll still have to be away some afternoons," he reasoned. "At least until this merger I'm working on is finalized. And I'd have to pay a sitter anyway. You're good for the girls. You're good for me. It's a perfect solution."

"What about…" She motioned between them. "What about—"

"The fact that it's taking more self-control than I thought I had not to reach for you again?"

He had to have more of whatever had just happened. He had to have her in his arms again, coming apart, moaning as she returned every kiss, every stroke of his hands.

Each moment with Bailey, each new thing he learned about her, made him need more.

"Derrick, I…" She glanced from his tailored suit to the jeans and T-shirt she seemed to wear 24/7. "I'm not—"

"Interested?" He was crowding her again. Rubbing his thumb across her lips. "You're going to have a hard time making me believe that one."

"Of course I'm interested! What woman wouldn't be? Look at you." She turned the hand that gestured toward him on herself. "Look at me."

"My pleasure." He let his gaze linger on every curve as it slid down her petite frame, then treated himself to seconds on the way back up. His body responded with a jolt that was even harder to control when he found her nervously licking her lips once he was done. "Now what?"

"Now, nothing." She edged away. "We both know I'm out of your league. I don't—"

"My league of football groupies?" Of course, the Mighty DC would have legions of them. "Or the local socialites who think my money's a fancy new toy to play with, right up until they realize that my two girls come with the package? How about my ex-wife's league—riding the wheels off one relationship, then sprinting to the next before the dust settles? Be careful. Telling me you can't hang with women like that only makes you more attractive."

The teakettle began to whistle. He reached for the switch, his body brushing Bailey's, as he set the kettle aside to cool. Leaning a hand against the counter, he waited for her to shy away again.

She didn't.

"If you don't want me to kiss you again, I'll understand," he said. "But—"

Her hand covered his.

"I've wanted to kiss you since I was fourteen years old. I've wanted to kiss you since you stumbled into Drayton's office last week and told me to butt out of your problems with Leslie."

He tried to swallow his chuckle.

Not a chance.

"Wanna guess where I'd rather see your butt now?" he asked.

She snorted, batting his shoulder, then reached for his hand again.

His stomach clenched when her expression sobered. If she dumped him, after telling him she'd wanted him since they were kids, he'd finish losing what was left of his mind.

"This is all moving a little fast for me, Derrick." Her fingers whispered across his as she slid her hand away. "My life is already confusing enough. I just… I can't do this right now."

"Then we'll slow things down." Whatever it took, for as long as it took, for her to trust how completely she'd captivated him. "But Leslie—"

"Of course. I'll spend whatever time I can spare with her." Bailey crossed her arms. "But don't you dare offer to pay me a dime."

"What about the time we'll be taking away from your work?"

"It won't make any difference." Her shoulders sunk. "If we can't secure another line of credit with the bank, we're going to lose the inn."

CHAPTER NINE

"A COOKOUT?" Leslie sputtered that afternoon, sweeping the broom faster across the convenience store's tiled floor.

"According to your dad, the alumni social's this Saturday, before the Western–Langston game." Why hadn't Bailey kept her mouth shut and let Derrick break the news? "He asked if I'd mind coming along and keeping an eye on you and your sister."

"You mean keep us out of trouble while he works." Leslie handed over the broom, squatting to hold the dustpan so Bailey could do the honors. "His boss is an alum. The guy's the father of some high school football buddy, and a partner in Dad's firm. Dad'll spend the whole time shaking hands and laughing that way he does when he doesn't mean it, while he's totally ignoring us. He and Mom are the life of every party. My sister and I come along as part of the act."

Bailey swallowed the memory of her and Derrick's very private party that morning.

Focus on the kid, Bailey, not the man you can't deal with right now.

"I think your dad really wants you and Savannah there. Why go through the trouble of making sure I could hang out with you guys, if he didn't?"

"We're like those stupid trophies his lawyer friends drool over when they come to the house. Or the jewelry my mom wears, like, everywhere. He shows us off, so everyone sees what a big deal he is. We're good for business."

"So you figured you'd make sure you aren't anything he'd want to show off, is that it?" The girl's juvie-or-bust behavior suddenly made a whole lot more sense.

"Why not? If he's ashamed of me, maybe he'll stop dragging me around to all these places I don't want to go, to do all that boring stuff I don't want to do."

"What exactly *do* you want to do? And don't even try to convince me wearing trashy clothes and getting into trouble on purpose are your new leases on life."

Leslie rolled her eyes.

The tank top and skinny jeans the girl wore were almost conservative, compared to her other getups.

"The clothes are mostly my friend Ginger's," Leslie admitted. "And smoking pot in her basement was just for—"

"Attention, I got that. You've still wasted an awful lot of time on this bad-girl-gone-wild act of yours, just so you could piss off your dad. Why not spend the time doing something you actually like to do?"

For once there was no smart-aleck comeback.

"Unless you're telling me you've got nothing better to do," Bailey pressed. "In that case, you have a bright future ahead of you in the field of convenience-store hospitality. But I'm guessing a smart kid like you isn't that much of a quitter. There's got to be something else. Come on, spill. What would you rather be doing than working here every afternoon?"

"Playing softball, all right!" Leslie shoved the dustpan into Bailey's stomach, then crossed her arms, daring Bailey to laugh. "I've wanted to play for years, but my mom always had a cow when I brought it up. She kept taking me to check out cheerleading practices instead. The thought of one of her daughters sweating away under a helmet was closed for discussion. When we moved out here, I figured maybe I'd have my chance. My mom's not around, and my dad loves sports…."

"He was almost as good at baseball as he was at football in high school." And Bailey had been there for every inning of his last season. "I'm sure your dad would be thrilled to know you're interested in playing."

How could Derrick not have jumped all over this? Team sports every afternoon would give a girl with Leslie's talent for getting into trouble something constructive to do.

Leslie kicked at the pile of dust she hadn't yet scooped up.

"When we first moved here, I'd go watch the Langston High team in the afternoons. They practiced every day. I even decided I wanted to catch, or pitch."

"But?"

"*But*, the coach recognized me one day. He played baseball with my dad or something. Called him a legend. He told me that if I'd like to play when I got to Langston, to tell my dad there would always be a spot for me, if he'd be willing to help out with the pitching staff sometimes."

"And you wouldn't want him to?"

"So everyone can fall all over themselves sucking up to him, and totally ignore *me?* I don't care how much I want to play, assuming I'm even any good. If my dad shows up, it'll be all about him. It's always all about him or my mom. Don't you get it? That's the way our family works."

Leslie ran toward the storeroom, leaving Bailey with the dustpan and the memory of how envious Derrick had seemed of her simple life. Her closeness with her grandmother. The depth of respect and understanding that took even Bailey by surprise some days.

If she had nothing else, she'd always had a family to make her feel loved. Derrick's relationship with his dad had been all football, all the time. Was it any wonder he was struggling to connect with his own kids in any meaningful way?

Saturday's alumni social at the Western–Langston game promised to be a Derrick Cavenaugh lovefest. For his daughter, it was a minefield waiting to explode.

"She better be working back there," Drayton grumped from the register.

Cranky pants had just arrived to cover the six-to-closing shift.

Sally had called in sick, and Bailey had already agreed to take Leslie home and spare Savannah's babysitter until Derrick could break free of some last-minute conference call.

"Leslie's working the whole time she's here. A whole lot harder than Scott ever does." Bailey didn't waste the energy elaborating on why the lazy kid was a waste of Drayton's feeble payroll. "You should consider letting her off the hook after this week. She's done her time."

"She's done when I say she's done." Her boss puffed out his chest. "If you think Scott's not pulling his weight, you do something about it. You wanted a manager's salary. Handle it, or cover the extra work yourself."

"Oh, I *have* worked extra hours. I've covered your financial butt for years, free of charge, because you're too cheap to pay an accountant, and I was desperate to keep my job. Finally paying me my due doesn't mean I'm picking up after other employees you don't expect to do their work. Set my schedule up two weeks in advance, same as always. I'll be here for as many shifts as you need. And I'll gladly supervise Leslie Cavenaugh for as long as her father lets you keep her under your thumb. But that's it."

"I'm the owner here. I decide what your responsibilities are." Drayton's bushy eyebrows shot up as he blustered. The weekend artists who painted caricatures in front of the Museum for Cartoon Art in SOMA would have had a field day with the image. "You're getting a little too uppity for your own good lately."

"Then fire me."

She didn't have a clue what she'd do if he did. But she'd put up with Drayton's nonsense for years. Until Margo had offered her a job, she'd never tried to find anything better. It had been essential that she keep her head down and work.

Or maybe it had just been easier.

"Pay me an honest wage for an honest day's work," she demanded, leaving neither Drayton nor herself an out. "Or find someone else to oversee the things around here you don't think are worth your time."

"How about investigating theft?" He rounded the desk. "Honest enough work for you to spend your precious time on?"

"What are you talking about?"

"There are things missing. Merchandise I can't find."

"In this immaculately organized place? You've got to be kidding." Things regularly went missing for weeks at a time, before they appeared again.

"I'm talking about inventory I received from vendors last Monday. We're short two cases of wine coolers and several twelve-packs of beer." He nodded his head after Leslie. "And I want to know where it all went."

"What are you getting at?" Bailey's stomach took a dive for her toes.

"You know exactly what I'm getting at." He fished his cigarettes and lighter from his shirt pocket. "And it's your job now to take care of it. I want my merchandise back. I want whoever's taken it in jail. And until that happens, the Cavenaugh girl is going to keep working here, or she goes before the judge. Now cover the register. I need a smoke."

Too stunned to remind him that she and Leslie were supposed to have left five minutes ago, Bailey perched on the stool behind the counter.

There was no way Leslie was stealing from the Stop Right.

She was a good kid, who seemed more inclined every day to clean up her act. Maybe even to give her dad another chance. Besides, they were together almost every second she was in the store. There was no way she'd have the chance to smuggle that much stuff out of there.

Bailey looked down the hall to the storeroom that Leslie had disappeared into.

Was there?

"YES, SIR," Derrick said to Reynolds-Allied's VP of acquisitions, who'd phoned into the conference room from his vacation in Maui. "We'll have everything ready by the end of September."

Closing this merger would secure his business footing in San Francisco. After working seventy hours a week for over a year, he would finally be a junior partner, and in a position to take some downtime with his family. To start making up for all that he'd missed.

Except the pep talk that usually got him through the day wasn't working tonight.

Bailey would be with the girls by now, no doubt looking gorgeous and just right in his home. They'd be downing the pizza and soda she'd said she'd order. Finishing homework, maybe playing a game afterward. Savannah had been on his case to break out the board games, but there'd never been time.

In the last year, he'd had to bring more work home than he could possibly get done. Details and research that had to be dealt with, without anyone in his office seeing him sweat.

The only people who got to see him sweat were the ones he let down at home.

"Derrick?" Spencer Hastings prompted from the head of the conference table. "Are you with us?"

Expectant expressions from around the room locked onto Derrick. Someone had directed a question at him, probably more than once.

"Like I said." He tried to find his golden-boy grin, but it wouldn't come. "We'll be ready to close the deal on time."

"Mr. Capry was asking about the next conference call." Spencer raised an eyebrow. "He'll be on an island cruise with his family all weekend."

"Then let's regroup on Monday. I have another meeting with—"

A knock on the door was followed by Derrick's secretary poking her head inside.

"I said no interruptions, Margery."

"Yes, sir. But I have an emergency call for you from home."

Spencer jerked his head toward the hallway, waving Derrick off.

"I have a lunch meeting with your staff tomorrow, Mr. Capry," Derrick finished as he stood. "Then I'll spend the weekend making sure we're on track on our end. By Monday, I'll have another update ready. Say around one in the afternoon?"

"Sounds good," Capry agreed. "Looking forward to hearing from you."

"Derrick's going to have to step away now." Spencer added as Derrick grabbed his portfolio and hurried out.

"She wouldn't tell me what it was about." Margery had to hustle to keep up with him in the hall. "Just that she was your wife, and it was critical—"

"My wife!" He stopped so fast, he probably left skid marks in the carpet.

"She said she had too speak to you right away." Margery's eyes widened as Derrick's fury made its way into his expression. "Something about it being life or death."

"With my ex-wife, it's always life or death."

He patted his secretary's shoulder. It wasn't Margery's fault he'd never considered the possibility that his ex might try to reach him at work. Amanda had his cell number. But when they'd moved to the West Coast, he'd stopped taking her calls anywhere but home.

"Don't worry about it," he said. "I'll take it in my office."

"Line three," Margery called after him.

Dropping his portfolio onto the desk, he loosened

his tie, then ran shaking fingers through his hair. Feeling ready to do violence wasn't the best way to approach talking with the mother of his children for the first time in over a month.

He punched line three so hard, the phone's base rattled across the desk.

"Amanda. How's the house hunting going?"

"Frustrating." Her long-suffering tone said he'd never know how much. "You wouldn't believe what they're asking for Buckhead property these days. And Rodney won't go any higher than two-point-five, when we could obviously afford so much more."

"Yeah. Two million isn't really your style, is it?"

The new Mrs. Canton sounded in rare form.

It shouldn't be so entertaining, thinking of his former college roommate getting up close and personal with the money pit that Amanda had become since they'd all met at the University of Georgia.

"I'm sure you'll get what you want in the end," Derrick commiserated.

Whatever that was.

Derrick sat, some of the bitterness he'd carried around for so long softening to gratitude.

Amanda's out-of-control consumption was no longer his problem. Neither was the low self-esteem that had taken root in high school, when no matter how pretty or popular she became, Amanda's parents were never going to love her enough to give loving each other a serious try. Still, they'd stayed together, torturing each other and their only child, refusing to expose themselves to the public embarrassment of a high-profile divorce.

Amanda's bank executive father committed suicide during her and Derrick's second year at UGA. Derrick proposed to her only a few months later, after she revealed she was pregnant. And he'd worked like a dog for the next thirteen years to give her whatever she'd thought she needed to be happy.

Now it was Rodney's turn.

"I'm planning a bit of a break from everything, while Rodney's on the road this weekend," Amanda announced.

"That should be fun." She'd always loved to travel, especially for his college games, when being at his side garnered her the elevated status she craved. "When do you leave for New York?"

"Actually, I'm not going with Rodney. He'll have all that pre- and post-game press to do. And I think they're going to do a sound bite for a Monday night football commercial. I'd just be bored."

Bored?

Derrick's newfound relief at finally being off his ex-wife's radar—even though that meant his girls were, too—evaporated.

"And?" he asked.

"And, I got the e-mail about the alumni social

before Saturday night's game. I thought it might be a good time to catch up with Leslie and Savannah and some of our old San Francisco friends."

Rodney was going to New York without her.

Amanda was looking at a lonely weekend in Atlanta and—

"You already have your flight scheduled, don't you?"

"I'll be there in the morning."

Derrick yanked his tie open another inch. "This isn't a good time, Amanda." It was the worst possible time for her to remember she had obligations outside of her new life. "I'm buried in a deal that's been busting my hump all year, and—"

"But the e-mail said you were bringing the girls to the game."

"Yes." And what did it say that Amanda had had to find that out through an alumni bulletin? "But I've got someone coming to hang with Leslie and Savannah, and then to watch them later in the evening when I have to get back to work."

"So let your sitter go, and I'll take the girls for the night."

"Amanda, you know as well as I do that you'll hook up with friends and want to go out after the game." The girls would be left disappointed because the mother they'd been told had flown cross-country to spend time with them would have ditched them all over again.

"Then we'll call your sitter and ask her to pick them up," Amanda reasoned.

"She's a friend, not a babysitter. And she's not at my beck and call. She has a busy life of her own."

"Is it Selena again? I swear, if I didn't know that woman had sworn off marriage years ago, I'd think she had her eye on you."

"No, it's someone who was several years behind us at Western."

"I didn't think there was anyone from Western you kept up with besides Selena. Do I know her?"

"Her name is Bailey Greenwood." And *he* didn't know her nearly as well as he'd like to. "I've already asked her to rearrange her plans for us. She's gone out of her way to help with Leslie lately, and—"

"Help with Leslie?"

"It's been a little rough for her since we moved." And Amanda had been oblivious. "I've left you several messages."

"I've been—"

"Busy, I know. And while you were enjoying your new life, I've had to get some help, so I can take care of the girls while I get things off the ground at my new firm."

"And as usual, your work is a far more important priority than my life." The image of an exotic bird ruffling its gaudy feathers accompanied Amanda's tone. "I raised those girls while you were *getting things off the ground* here. I'm not going to apologize for taking some time to focus on me."

"I'm not asking for an apology. Just don't come to San Francisco thinking you can disrupt our schedule, without knowing what you're walking into."

And bringing her up to speed would pretty much blow away the weekend he'd already committed to finalizing details on the Reynolds-Allied deal.

"What exactly am I walking into? The girls were fine when I left them with you."

"Yes, they were elated that their mom was happy again. That kind of wore off after the first month or so of not seeing you. They're finally settling in here, but it's been a rocky year. Especially for Leslie."

"She's twelve. Twelve-year-olds overdramatize everything. I know I did at that age."

Did she honestly believe comparing Leslie's self-centered phase to herself would win her points?

"She misses you," he said, trying to remember his own part in all this. "Hell, she misses *me*. Both girls do. It's not like I've been able to give them all they need since we got here."

"Welcome to single parenthood, Derrick. There's never enough time."

"No, there's not." But he was going to keep fighting, regardless. "So you'll understand why I have to get back to work. Call me on my cell when you get into town. Let me know where you end up staying, and the girls and I will meet you for dinner."

A long pause followed.

He didn't want her in his house, even though they had an extra bedroom he used as his home gym and office.

He'd never deny Leslie and Savannah whatever time their mother wanted. No matter that each encounter left him with the urge to drink. Heavily.

But after the last year of limbo, there were going to be some boundaries. Savannah would want to spend every waking moment with her mommy. But Leslie...

Lord knew how Leslie was going to react to Amanda's reappearance.

"Then I guess I'll be in touch tomorrow." Amanda sounded hurt, but he was finding it hard to care.

All he could see were his kids' tears, every time their mother had bailed on a planned visit.

"I'm sure the girls will be thrilled to see you." He hadn't finished speaking before Amanda hung up.

Cavenaugh family time was going to be a thrill a minute this weekend.

And thanks to him pushing Bailey to get more involved in their lives, the woman he'd held in his arms that morning was going to be right in the middle of the drama.

CHAPTER TEN

"I DIDN'T DO IT!" Leslie jumped up from the couch to glare at the two adults in front of her.

Her dad hadn't stopped pacing since he'd gotten home half an hour ago, and Bailey was frowning right along with him.

"You can understand why Mr. Drayton would be suspicious, can't you?" Her dad looked wrecked, even more than usual. He had since he'd walked in the door, even before Bailey's bombshell about the missing stuff at the store. "You're working there because you were caught stealing once before."

"I told Drayton that she couldn't have taken anything," Bailey said.

Because Bailey believed Leslie wouldn't have done it? Or because she'd kept an eagle eye on her, while she'd pretended to be Leslie's friend?

"Don't do me any favors." Leslie bolted for her room.

Wasn't this exactly the kind of trouble she'd hoped to cause when she hooked up with Ginger? Why she hadn't told anyone when Ginger and Brett lifted the stuff from the storeroom? The whole point of the last year had been to cause enough trouble so her dad would let her go back to Atlanta. Or at least notice that she was alive.

What were the chances he'd work the night away now, buried in the stupid papers he dragged home in his briefcase every day?

Except she kept remembering how he'd hung out and watched a movie last night. How much she'd rather be doing that right now, instead of yelling at him until it made her sick to her stomach from all the pizza she'd eaten. She'd give anything to hear him say that he believed her, too, the way Bailey had.

Even if he didn't really mean it.

"What are they talking about?" Savannah asked from her bedroom's doorway. Some lame boy band that Leslie used to drool over was blasting from the kid's CD player.

"Me."

Leslie didn't stop.

Her sister and everyone else in town would know the details soon enough. Leslie was the center of attention, most importantly her father's.

Mission accomplished.

But as she shut herself in her room, she'd never felt more alone.

"I DOUBLE-CHECKED the inventory," Bailey said. "We're definitely missing several cases of drinks, all of them alcoholic. But I refuse to believe Leslie had anything to do with it."

"Of course she didn't." Derrick sounded every bit the protective father, but the slight hesitation before he'd spoken left room for the kind of doubt his daughter had already picked up on.

"Drayton has no proof it was Leslie," Bailey reasoned. Otherwise, he'd already have called the police. "I'll figure out where everything went."

"With what time?" Derrick picked at the fringe on one of the sofa's throw pillows, then flung it across the room. Bracing his hands on his hips, he inspected the tips of his shined-to-perfection dress shoes. "And believe it or not, I have an even more pressing problem we need to talk about."

Here it comes.

She'd intentionally taken her hair down after driving Leslie home and ordering pizza for dinner, because Derrick had liked it down that morning. She'd had a blast, hanging out with the girls. Helping people she cared about, instead of serving strangers at the store or the bistro. Looking forward to Derrick coming home and smiling at her again.

Now, the embarrassed, uncomfortable expression on his face said it all. He'd had the whole day to come to his senses.

"Look, you don't have to say any more." And she didn't think she could hear it. She scooped up her bag and headed for the door. "I understand—"

His touch stopped her. He tugged until she turned to face him.

"It's been hell, not being able to touch you all day." He pulled her closer, far too gently for a man of his size. He cradled her head to his chest, making her feel slight and feminine. Cherished. "No matter what, you have to believe that, Bailey. You've gotten under my skin so fast, I can't seem to stop it."

"But?" Why was he making this even harder?

"*But,* you might have been better off if I had."

Her head came off his shoulder. She shivered at the loss of sensation.

"*I* might be better off?"

"Amanda's flying in for the Weston–Langston game." His hands fell away. "She'll be here sometime tomorrow."

Bailey actually smiled in relief, then the reality of what the next few days would be like for Derrick and the girls sunk in.

"Let me guess," she surmised. "Amanda isn't going to be happy to find Leslie having so many problems."

"Or finding you right here in the middle of it with us, saving the day, after she's made a point of not caring what her kids were doing for over a year."

"I'm not saving anything." Bailey waved away his compliment.

"You're quite possibly the only reason I've gotten through this week without losing it. You've been a godsend for Leslie, and Amanda's not used to being upstaged."

In the middle of it with us...

A godsend...

She didn't notice the tears in her eyes, until they'd blurred him away.

"Bailey?"

She stepped back into his arms, reaching for him, even though it was still a bad idea.

"You make me sound so..." She wasn't sure, except that she loved whatever it was he made her sound like.

"What?" he asked.

"Different." She hated admitting it. "Different than I've thought of myself in a long time."

"Then it's about time someone woke you up." His eyes had always been a gorgeous gray. He curled a hand in her hair, and they deepened into something closer to black. His touch was something Bailey needed, whether she wanted to admit it or not. "And I don't want anything that happens this weekend to mess with that. My ex-wife—"

"Is child's play compared to Larry Drayton. I can handle her." At the moment, Bailey felt like she could handle anything. "It's your daughter I'm worried about. Leslie's still so angry, and she…"

Bailey shook her head, unable to finish. He needed to hear the truth, to deal with it. But saying it would hurt him, and she'd done enough of that when she'd first stuck her nose into his and Leslie's relationship.

"She doesn't think either her mother or I care about her." Derrick's shoulders stiffened beneath her touch.

"You didn't even give her a chance to explain just now. How often do you two actually talk?"

"I know I'm working too many hours still. It'll be hard for the girls for just a little while longer, but—"

"It's not just the hours you work. You hold so much in." She smoothed a hand over a rock-solid shoulder. "You're such a guy. I've seen you agonize over not being able to give your kids everything they need. I've seen you ask for help, probably for the first time in your life. But have you let your daughters know how hard you're trying, how much you wish you could do more? Have you given Leslie a chance to tell you how she feels, without her having to scream it at you?"

"I'm doing the best I can." He didn't sound like he believed a word he was saying. "Leslie's upset about—"

"She's not upset." Bailey knew nothing about the sacrifices single parents had to make. But discouraged, disillusioned young girls, she understood. "She's got a plan. And she's willing to self-destruct to get what she wants."

"And what exactly is that!" The warmth was gone from his eyes. "Since this is all my fault, and Leslie won't tell me what she needs, suppose *you* tell me what magical thing I can do to fix this for my child."

If it were any other man towering over her, Bailey would have taken a step back. Instead, she stood on her tiptoes and kissed Derrick's cheek.

"Stop trying to fix things for a minute, and listen to your daughter," she said on her way out the door.

She had an avalanche of problems of her own to deal with tomorrow. A morning's worth of work around the inn before meeting Leslie at the Stop Right, including entertaining the IRS auditor who was coming to discuss the discrepancies he'd found. Then she was closing at Margo's, because no one else had wanted to work on a Friday night.

That was her life. Being careful to always be around. Being willing to work when others couldn't. She was a paragon of making safe, dependable choices.

Except as she pulled out of the driveway, she wanted to be back in Derrick's arms, throwing caution to the wind and kissing him as if it could be the beginning of something real. A dream that would last, instead of evaporating like all the rest.

She glanced back.

Derrick was standing silhouetted in the doorway, looking so alone. Lost.

Almost afraid of what might happen next.

She knew exactly how he felt.

"WHAT NOW!" Bailey ranted just before nine the following morning.

The second floor suite's shower was backed up, and their newlyweds' toilet had overflowed before breakfast. Setting aside the plunger with a growl, wiping her hands on her overalls as she left the shower to drown in its own contrariness, she checked her watch and stomped downstairs in response to the front-desk buzzer.

A note beside the device invited visitors to press it to speak to the staff. Most people ignored both note and buzzer, except when Bailey was the only *staff* available, as was the case today.

Leave it to the IRS auditor to come the morning that Grams had gone in for an emergency root canal. And he was forty-five minutes early, to boot.

Correction, *she* was forty-five minutes early.

When Bailey reached the bottom of the stairs, a smartly dressed woman was waiting less than patiently in the foyer. And she was still buzzing.

From the looks of her designer everything, right down to the hair color and highlights that could only be achieved after grueling hours at the spa, civil servants were doing pretty well for themselves these days. Then she turned at the sound of Bailey's approach. And instead of an IRS auditor, Bailey found herself staring openmouthed at a Western High School homecoming queen, in all her grown-up glory.

"Amanda!" She checked her watch again. "What are you doing here?" The hint of horror in her voice made her wince. "I mean, Derrick mentioned you were coming for the game, but it's so early in the morning. And, well, I don't usually dress like this...well, actually I do..." She wiped at the wet patches running down her front, then smoothed her bangs back and flipped her ponytail, silently coveting the other woman's neatly coifed curls. "I don't always look like a drowned rat."

Stop it!

Stop talking like a clueless freshman, groveling at the feet of the most popular girl in the senior class.

Clearing her throat, she extended her hand.

"What brings you to the Gables?"

The question was as close to polite chitchat as Bailey could manage.

Amanda had contributed more than her share to Leslie's heartache and Derrick's out-of-control home life. And the woman's appearance at the inn, her glance of dismay at her less-than-glamorous sur-roundings, was already getting on Bailey's last nerve. The sooner they got this over with, the better.

"Why, I'm here for a room. One with a private bath, of course."

Okay, so much for better.

"I thought you'd be—"

"Staying with my family?" If Amanda's megawatt smile stretched any wider, she'd be nothing but gums. "Derrick thought it would be best that I not disrupt the girls' routine."

"So he sent you right on over, did he?"

"Actually, no. He mentioned that you were baby-sitting Leslie in the afternoons, and I must admit I was intrigued. Your name sounded familiar, but I couldn't quite place you. The alumni Web site included a link to this old place, and I just couldn't resist, once I saw how quaint it was. And you're so close to Derrick's, it's like it was meant to be."

Bailey mentally decoded. She was a nobody in high school. Her run-down bed and breakfast was convenient, because it was two blocks from Amanda's ex and their girls. But that didn't change the fact that Bailey was still a nobody, and Amanda was here to make sure she didn't forget it.

She stepped behind the desk.

"Let me see what we have available on such short notice. It's going to be a very busy weekend, I'm afraid."

It wasn't a complete lie. They were expecting quite a few guests, thanks to the Western–Langston grudge match and the ad she'd placed on the alumni Web site. Still, there were several rooms available, not that Amanda needed to know that.

"We only have one suite left. Unfortunately, its plumbing is currently on strike, and I haven't quite beat the shower into submission. But if I can't show it who's boss by tonight, I promise I'll call in a plumber. The original second-floor bathroom in the hall is perfectly lovely, though. You could use that in the meantime."

"*Share* a bathroom." Someone who'd been asked to strip naked and run through the halls couldn't have looked more shocked. "What kind of hotel is this?"

"A turn-of-the-century Victorian, that doesn't take kindly to me rooting around in its pipes. I'm sorry I can't offer anything more accommodating." Bailey paused. When lightning didn't strike, she took it as permission to proceed. "But I can understand what you mean, about wanting to be as close as possible to your girls. If I were in your shoes, I'd do just about anything to have as much time with them as I could get."

"Yes, I miss them terribly." Amanda's eyes narrowed, but not her smile. "The room sounds lovely. Do you have someone who can take up my bags?"

She motioned to the two suitcases left just inside the door—for a three-day weekend.

"That would be me."

An idiot, who'd shamed the last woman on earth

she wanted under her roof into treating her like the hired help. All because she was feeling ridiculously jealous of someone she barely remembered. A woman Derrick had divorced over a year ago.

"As soon as I take an imprint of your credit card," she added. "I'll show you right up."

Amanda pulled a Gucci wallet from her Gucci purse, and removed a platinum card from its nest of friends.

"Um, we don't take American Express," Bailey said.

"Of course you don't." Amanda's empty laugh was the same put-down it had been when they were kids.

And let the good times roll!

CHAPTER ELEVEN

"HOW ARE THINGS going with Bailey?" Selena asked from where she stood beside Derrick at Langston High stadium.

They'd just gotten up from one of the picnic tables the alumni were still milling around, even though the football game had already begun. So far, Amanda was a no-show—she'd spent the day shopping and catching up with friends—and Derrick was trying unsuccessfully not to be grateful.

"Bailey's great with the kids." He couldn't tear his eyes away from the sight of Savannah and Leslie near the bleachers, laughing as Bailey set down a hot dog, licked ketchup off her thumb and in the process smeared a dab on her nose.

"Yes, I can see that." Selena quite frequently saw way too much. "But I was asking about the two of you, not the girls."

A recent client passed by.

"Great to see you here," Michael Brody said.

Derrick smiled and shook the man's hand. "It's great to finally make one of these things."

And it was.

His girls were having a blast.

What's a football game without hot dogs, Bailey had insisted when they began clamoring for something from the concession stand, labeling the *adult* food catered in for the alumni social too boring to choke down. Left to his own devices, Derrick would have done what he'd assumed was *fatherly,* and refused to indulge them. But thanks to Bailey, the girls were now content to hang out while he played the see-and-be-seen game that was part of his job. And as an added bonus, he got to keep glancing Bailey's way, writing it off as being an observant father.

As a rule, he didn't attend football games. Or any other sporting event anymore. The reality of what he'd never do again was still too raw for him to be able to play rec league sports or enjoy being a spectator. Instead, he worked out daily at home, in private, with the free weights and elliptical glide machine in his guest room.

Selena's eyebrow raised at his refusal to answer her question.

"Bailey and I aren't *going* anywhere right now," he explained. "We both have too much else going on."

His friend chuckled as her son and their newly

adopted dog bounded up to the girls. The mutt made a leap for Bailey's food. With a whoop, Bailey jumped up from the bleachers, and dropped her hot dog down her front, earning her even more doggy affection as the creature tried to lick up every crumb.

"Hope you like the smell of dog slobber, DC," a purring voice said from behind him. Amanda, the only person on the planet who still called him DC, looped her arm through his elbow. "That one seems a little slimy, even for you."

"Speaking of too much," Selena said under her breath. For the crowd of people now looking their way, she added, "Amanda, you're looking wonderful."

Amanda's strategically too-tight Western High jersey and larger-than-necessary diamond earrings were just enough *trying too hard* to guarantee her the bevy of compliments she adored.

"And you're as refreshingly colorful as ever." Amanda air-kissed Selena's right cheek. "You artists live such charmed lives, getting away with wearing things the rest of us wouldn't dream of throwing together."

Selena responded by clasping her hands in front of her, when she'd offered everyone else from their graduating class enthusiastic hugs. She nodded toward the bleachers.

"Slimy or not—" her smile turned genuine as Bailey dropped to her knees to wrestle with the dog, the girls following "—that's the most fun I've seen your kids have in months."

Amanda brought her hand to her throat at the sight of her offspring rolling in the dirt, but she managed an indulgent chuckle for Selena.

"Girls will be girls." She looked from Bailey to Derrick. "I see why you're concerned about Leslie. She's dressed even worse today than yesterday."

They'd met for dinner last night, after Amanda had called from, of all places, the Gables Inn. Driving up to the Greenwoods' home to see Amanda, instead of Bailey, had been hard enough. Watching Savannah's sprint to hug her mother end awkwardly, as Amanda scrutinized the T-shirt and jeans Leslie had decided to wear to school that day, had been agony.

"She looks great." Selena's smile was so brittle, she'd bite a hole in her cheek if she wasn't careful. "Derrick couldn't get her out of the nightmare outfits she's been wearing. But after only a few days of working with Bailey, the girl's made the decision to change on her own."

Derrick grimaced as Amanda's acrylic nails dug into the arm she still held.

"Nightmare outfits?" she asked under her breath.

"Why don't we wait until tomorrow to talk about everything." Until they were away from the stadium crawling with colleagues and neighbors, including

Spencer Hastings and Douglas Capry's second in command, Trent Layton.

"Everything?" she demanded in the same condescending tone with which she used to scold the kids.

"Everything you've missed while you've been taking your year-long honeymoon."

Screw being talked to like a child. And screw the fact that all eyes were clearly riveted to their conversation.

"Now look…" Amanda lifted a finger, a freshly lacquered, magenta nail, primed and ready.

He shoved it away.

"Tomorrow. We're not doing this now, not in front of our kids. Not because you had better things to do all day than spend time with them."

He removed Amanda's arm and steered Selena toward the bleachers.

Selena's twelve-year-old, Drew, was trying to control his beast. Leslie and Savannah's giggles were driving the canine's yips to ear-splitting decibels. And in the middle of it all was Bailey, having what looked like the time of her life, as if she were right where she belonged.

Grass-stained, her hair pulled free from its ponytail, her eyes sparkling up at him from the most beautiful, makeup-free face he'd ever seen, she was every honest, genuine thing Amanda wasn't.

"You're right," Selena said. She was once again

watching him watch Bailey. "She's definitely great with the kids."

Derrick looked over his shoulder.

Amanda was flipping her hair and laughing at something Spencer Hastings was saying. Turning back to where Bailey had pushed herself to her feet and was helping the girls to theirs, he lost his heart right then and there.

"She's great, period," he said to his friend.

Selena's expression warmed with approval.

"Sounds to me like the *Mighty DC* is finally ready to play ball again."

"COME ON, GIRLS, wrestling time's over," Leslie's mom insisted.

It had taken the woman ten minutes to work her way through her crowd of admirers and reach the bleachers.

"Mommy!" Savannah squealed and threw her arms around their mother.

Leslie had known their undignified doggie display would grab *Queen Amanda's* attention faster than anything else. But the plan had been to ignore their mom, once she reached them.

She and Savannah were going to have to have another talk.

No way were they forgetting that their mom had been a no-show for the last year, while she fooled around with her new husband. And popping in from out of the blue to party with her high school friends and, as an afterthought, play the doting mom for the crowd, was worse than not showing at all.

"Oh, honey." The woman brushed the grass and dirt from Savannah's back. *Appearance always matters, girls.* "That's better."

She hugged Savannah closer, once all the objectionable mess was gone.

Then she looked down at Leslie, who was petting the dog and trying to figure out why she'd wasted so much time pissing off her dad, in hopes of moving back home. One day of having *Amanda* in San Francisco was an instant replay of why all of them living in the same town was a really bad idea.

When Leslie's mother was around, everyone was miserable.

"Aren't you going to say hello?" her mom asked. "Or has your father let you forget all your manners?"

Leslie stood.

She walked to Bailey's side.

"Hello."

"Shoo!" Her mom used Savannah as a human shield against Axel. God forbid her designer jeans come into contact with muddy dog paws. "Shoo."

"He's just being friendly."

"He's filthy." Her mom grimaced at Leslie. "And he's not the only one."

"Come on, Axel." Selena grabbed a handful of dog collar. "Let's see if Drew and I can't find you a hot dog of your own."

"That animal's a menace," Leslie's mom bitched at her dad once the Milanos had left. "Leave it to Selena to pick up the mangiest mutt in San Francisco."

"He's a great dog!" Leslie shouted, not that she'd spent any real time with Axel.

Her mom didn't like pets, so they'd never owned one. Her mom didn't like her dad anymore, so she'd gone out and found herself a new husband. Her mom had been bored, so she'd dumped her children and let them be dragged to the other side of the country.

"Is there anything you *do* like anymore?" Leslie demanded. "Besides your clothes and your jewelry and your new fancy house and your new, improved football player boy-toy!"

"That's enough, Leslie," her dad warned. "This isn't the time or place for this."

"It never is."

The woman ruined everything that wasn't one hundred percent about her. And Leslie's dad had never done anything about it. He was too busy being a big successful lawyer to stop her.

Why did her parents think they had to be winners at everything, except *being parents?*

She caught her dad checking out the crowd, to see

if any of his superimportant clients were listening. What would they think, if she started a fight right then and there about the alcohol he was so sure she'd stolen from the Stop Right?

"I hate you both!" she yelled instead, taking off after the Milanos.

God, she'd rather hang out with a stinky dog than her own family.

"HAVE YOU SEEN LESLIE?" Bailey asked after jogging up to Selena and Drew. "She ran off a while ago, and I can't find her."

"You mean she's not clinging to her adoring mother?" With a quick glance down at her son, who was engrossed in his Game Boy, Selena sighed. "Sorry, but that woman's been nothing but trouble for years. If I hadn't already decided marriage wasn't for me, her and Derrick's relationship would have convinced me."

"It's been rough for everyone," Bailey agreed carefully. She didn't know Selena all that well, even if the honest, straightforward woman's friendship was something she'd very much like to have. "I think Leslie's feeling lost in the shuffle."

"She caught up to us a few minutes ago. She wouldn't say much, but she asked to take Axel for a walk." Selena's face shifted from angry to bemused. "In fact, she barely says anything to anyone these days, except you. The way you've bonded with her has been a huge help to Derrick."

Bailey smiled, even as a nagging suspicion took deeper root.

Just how tied to his daughter's well-being was Derrick's interest in her?

"Did you see which way they went?" she asked.

"Toward the concessions stand," Drew answered. "I think she wanted to get Axel another hot dog. Man, I bet he could eat a hundred of them!"

"Yeah?" Selena eyed her kid as if he'd lost his mind. "And you'll be helping me clean up each and every one that he upchucks in the loft tonight."

Drew shrugged and turned back to his game.

"Did Amanda really take a room at the Gables?" Selena shook her head at Bailey's brief nod. "That woman has no shame."

"We're trying to make her as comfortable as we can."

Actually, Bailey had dragged out repairs on the shower, burnt the woman's breakfast that morning and had run out of fabric softener when it came time to dry her sheets. Which just about made up for the fact that when Amanda returned from a day of shopping that afternoon, she'd asked Grams, whose face was still swollen from her root canal, to "run her shopping bags up to her room," while Amanda enjoyed the inn's complimentary afternoon tea.

For a woman who needed every paying guest she could get, Bailey had enjoyed making sure Amanda never returned to the inn to cause trouble.

"I get the impression Amanda's used to better accommodations," was all she let herself say to Selena.

"You can handle her. If the situation weren't so delicate, I might enjoy watching the show. Just don't let Amanda push you around, for Leslie's sake or anyone else's. Derrick's done that for too long. This whole move to San Francisco was his idea of how to protect the girls, without actually having to outright deal with what Amanda was doing."

For a man who'd been poised to make a living in one of the most violent sports there was, Derrick skirted confrontation in his personal life like a pro. And damn, if Bailey didn't feel a little like one of his latest avoidance techniques.

He'd seemed almost relieved when she'd offered to go after Leslie. After all, wasn't running interference with his kids the reason he'd asked her to come tonight?

"I'd better look for Leslie." She walked toward the concession area and caught sight of Derrick near the bleachers.

His back was conspicuously turned to where Amanda was showing Savannah off to the rest of the alumni.

Ten minutes later, Bailey had made a lap around the ball field, and still no Leslie. She'd asked everyone she knew if they'd seen the kid. No dice. She was hunting for the Milanos again when Derrick caught up with her.

"Someone said they saw a girl walking off with Axel a few minutes ago. Something about them heading toward the other side of the school."

"Of course! Why didn't I think of that?" Switching directions, Bailey didn't wait to see if he was following.

One thing she *had* found in the last half hour was her temper.

"Think of what?" He fell in step beside her.

"The baseball field."

"What? Leslie's middle school is three blocks away. She's never been to the fields here."

Bailey skidded to a halt.

Derrick, who'd charged several feet farther, had to stop and backtrack. She should stay out of this. She should send Derrick on alone, and add this night to her overflowing list of lessons learned.

Yesterday's IRS agent had been understanding but blunt—it was time to pay up. But instead of chaining herself to her computer, researching a way to convince First National to help the Gables out of its ten-thousand-dollar sinkhole, where was Bailey? Here, making it easier for Derrick to put off dealing with his own problems.

"Have you ever stopped to wonder why Leslie

assumes you don't care what she wants?" she demanded. "She told me she used to come over here almost every day after school to watch the softball team practice. She wants to play ball, Derrick. How can you not know that?"

He looked toward the fields.

"Because she never mentioned it. She's too busy hating me, to actually talk with me about anything! And I'm too buried under work to investigate the latest methods of forcing children to talk to their parents."

The shift in his mood wasn't unexpected. Neither was his favorite excuse. But Bailey was done helping him give up on being the kind of single parent she knew he could be.

"You don't have to *force* her." Every angry thing inside Bailey drained away, as she remembered the encouraging, supportive things he'd said to her. "Just ask questions that let Leslie know you're paying attention. Spend more time with her, time that doesn't involve three square meals a day, homework and bailing her out of jail. Find out what she likes, then find a way to like that, too."

When Bailey's own father had discovered her love for math and computers, they'd sat up nights going over the inn's books together. He'd let her research the new computer programs on the market, then had sat while she showed him how to automate the business's bookkeeping.

The family that geeks together, he'd always said, *stays together.*

"I'm doing the best I can," Derrick insisted.

"Finding ways to not interact with your children is what you're doing. You even brought me here tonight, so you wouldn't have to figure out what to do with them during the game. How long do you think it took Leslie to figure that out?"

"If you didn't want to stay with the girls, why didn't you—"

"*I* did want to stay with them. The question is, why didn't you? You were too busy avoiding Amanda and talking with your colleagues to even notice that Leslie was missing until I said something. And you think that's the best you can do?"

Derrick's head snapped back, as if she'd slapped him.

"Thanks for telling me about the baseball field. I think I can take it from here."

He stomped away, all-star shoulders stiff, his gait churning up the grass beneath his feet. He was going after his daughter himself—exactly what he should be doing. Now Bailey could put the night's confusion behind her and focus on the inn's finances, until she had to face Amanda over Grams's Sunday morning cinnamon rolls.

But an all-night, creative accounting extravaganza was the last thing she could stomach right now. Not until she was sure the stubborn single father she'd just told off found his equally stubborn child, and that both of them were okay.

"YOUR MOM AND I have been looking for you." Derrick sat on the bleachers beside his daughter.

He deserved Leslie's watery snort.

"Okay, Bailey and I have been looking for you." Even that wasn't totally accurate, but he couldn't stomach *the whole truth and nothing but,* with Bailey's painfully honest words still rattling him.

Leslie hadn't wanted to discuss Amanda being back. She wouldn't talk about the missing alcohol at the convenience store. And his excuse for not trying to get through to her again, and then again, was that he was a busy man with other things demanding his time.

It had been his excuse for so long, he hadn't realized what he was doing until Bailey called him on it.

"Look, I know this is tough," he finally said.

"Tough for *you,* you mean." Leslie kept rubbing the head of the dog panting at her feet. "Why don't you just ship us back to Atlanta with Mom?"

"Would you really rather be back there?" he asked, terrified of the answer.

"No!" her daughter spat.

"But you don't want to be here with me, either, do you?"

He'd have given anything for an eye roll. An

emotional outburst. Anything but the dead silence that followed.

Silence that in the past would have been his cue to pack the unhappy kid up and head home, to all the distractions that made the silence bearable.

But not this time.

"I'm sorry it took me so long to calm down Thursday night and realize you'd never have taken that stuff from the Stop Right."

Seconds ticked by as the oak trees surrounding the deserted backstop rustled in the darkness overhead.

"I thought about it," Leslie challenged. "I could have taken anything I wanted."

"Why would you want to?" Derrick gave himself credit for not shouting the question.

"Maybe I'm not as worried as you are about everyone thinking I'm perfect!" She shot up, but Derrick grabbed her wrist to stop her from running.

The dog backed under the bleachers, cowering.

"I'm not perfect. I *know* I'm not perfect." Derrick stood. He inhaled for a five count, the way he'd once prepared for the next play, the next snap. "But—"

"But *appearances are what matters,* right? Well, screw what your boss and those stupid people back there, and everyone but me and Savannah think!"

"So what *do* you think!" Axel was growling now. "Instead of punishing me, why not talk to me? Give me a chance to help."

"Like you talk to me?" Leslie yanked her hand away.

"I know I haven't listened to you and your sister enough. I haven't been home enough."

"But?" she spat at him.

"No. No *but*. I've made mistakes. I'd like the chance to make some of them right, but you have to meet me halfway. I want to start over, if you'd just tell me what I need to do."

Begging his child for parenting advice probably wasn't the best first step to take.

"You're such a loser." Leslie looked him up and down. "Do whatever you want. I don't care anymore."

She sprinted away, leaving behind the agitated dog, her last sentence so soft he'd almost missed it.

But he'd heard enough to know that his bright, determined child was giving up on him.

Just like Bailey was.

"SHE HAS NO BUSINESS HERE," Amanda insisted two hours later.

Still, Bailey hadn't been able to stay away from Derrick's house. Savannah was down the hall, safely tucked into bed, but no one had heard from Leslie in hours.

"She understands Leslie better than either one of us do." Derrick's reply was so sad, Bailey had to force herself not to offer the hug she sensed he needed. "She may be able to help us find her."

"She understands what?" Amanda twirled the enormous wedding set on her finger. "How to judge me for finally finding some happiness? You've already got that one covered, DC."

"I should go." Bailey made herself stand.

Having an outsider in the mix was only ratcheting up the tension Leslie would have to deal with, whenever she did come back.

"Stay, please." Derrick took her hand, touching her for the first time since the ball game. "For Leslie's sake."

He pulled out a chair at the opposite end of the table from his ex.

"I hear you're responsible for my daughter's new fashion sense," Amanda said, as Bailey sat again.

She finger-combed blond hair behind ears loaded with enough bling to spring the Gables from hock, twice over.

"If you mean it's Bailey's fault Leslie's no longer dressing like a preteen hooker?" Derrick said. "Then you're right on target."

Amanda gasped.

"Her clothes look like she's ready for gym class, not—"

"That's this week, after Bailey started helping out. Before then, Leslie looked like a backup singer in an MTV video."

"Since when!"

"Since she figured it was the best way to make her father so miserable, he'd decide to move back home." Bailey kept her gaze on the table as she spoke up. "Seems she figured the only way to make Derrick go back was to make him more miserable in San Francisco than he'd been in Atlanta."

"And you know this *how*, exactly?" Amanda demanded.

"Because I talked with her about it."

"And Leslie talked back," Derrick added. "Which is more than she's done with either one of us in a long time."

He stopped short of mentioning that Amanda wouldn't have been available, regardless.

The woman bristled all the same.

"I don't need the two of you telling me how to deal with my own child."

"Of course you do." Derrick drummed his fingers on the table. "We both do, or Leslie wouldn't have made the scene she did tonight, just to get our attention. Or run off to God knows where. Her behavior's grown progressively worse over the last year, but lately…"

"She's a very angry little girl," Bailey summed up.

"Angry at me, right?" Amanda cried. "I didn't fly out here to be ganged up on."

"No." Derrick sounded like his most sensible, lawyer self. "You supposedly came to spend time with your children, but you've barely managed to give them a few hours. Just like I barely managed to spend time with them for years. But I'm trying to make things right now. For the girls' sake, you need to, too."

"You refused to let me stay at the house."

"Because it's hard enough for them not to see you when you're halfway across town." His voice hardened with each word. "Imagine how confusing it would have been for the girls to see you coming and going through the front door at all hours of the day and night."

"I'm a good mother. I was their *only* full-time parent the first ten years of Leslie's life, when you were buried in law school and then building that nice little career of yours. I'm not going to apologize for finally expecting you to do your share of the work."

"I don't want an apology. I know I didn't do my part when the girls were younger. All I'm asking you to do is care—"

"Of course I care! They're my babies." If the tears that flooded Amanda's eyes were fake, the woman had taken manipulation to a whole new level.

Amanda fished a tissue from her designer clutch, then carefully dabbed at her perfectly made-up eyes.

"You care so much," he countered. "You have no idea that the atrocious clothing choices Leslie's finally stopped inflicting on everyone was just the start. She was caught shoplifting, and—"

"What?"

"And while she's been working off her crime under Bailey's supervision, she's been accused of stealing again, from the same store."

"There's no way my daughter would steal anything."

"I caught her red-handed," Bailey assured her. "Shoving the condoms that started all this under her shirt."

"Condoms!"

Bailey had walked out on Derrick after throwing that bit of info at him. Witnessing his ex-wife's reaction to the same news made Bailey feel even worse about being such a snot that day.

"I think she was doing it on a dare," she explained. "From what she's said, there's no boy in the picture, but there is this girl, Ginger, who's more than up for helping your daughter make as many mistakes as Leslie wants."

"Like the drugs," Derrick added.

"She's doing drugs?" Amanda covered her mouth with shaking fingers.

"Marijuana. I'd grounded her, because of the shoplifting." Derrick winced. "But then I left the girls with a sitter to get back to work, and—"

"What have you done!" Amanda blasted at him. "Leslie never got into trouble like this when she was with me."

"Because we hadn't totally ripped her world apart yet!"

Bailey's cell phone rang, relieving her from more in-her-face proof of how completely out of control Derrick's life really was.

"Hello?" She stepped into the kitchen.

"Honey," Grams said. "I have a friend of yours here I think Derrick will be relieved to see."

"Leslie?" Thank goodness.

"She rang the doorbell a few minutes ago and asked for you. Are you still at Derrick's place?"

"Yeah, I wanted to help find her." But instead, she'd added more fuel to Derrick and Amanda's relationship bonfire.

"Why don't I pack her up in the car and bring her over?"

"That would be great, Grams, thanks." She smiled as Derrick stepped into the kitchen, flashing him a thumbs-up sign as she hung up. "Leslie's at the Gables looking for me. My grandmother's bringing her over."

"Thank God."

Derrick pulled her into a hug that Bailey made herself slide away from.

"I should get going."

He followed her down the hall, away from the dining room. "I know I was a jerk earlier, and I know you're busy. But—"

"I've done everything I can for Leslie." Maybe too much. She was one more crutch he'd used to avoid dealing with his daughter. "I'll take care of things at the Stop Right until she's done there, but I don't think the rest of this is working."

"The rest of what?" He placed a palm on the front door to prevent her from opening it. "Spending more time with Leslie, or spending more time with me?"

"Either."

She brushed at her bangs.

After sharing so much space with the man's glamorous ex-wife, she was more conscious than ever of how long it had been since she'd put any thought into her own appearance. How long she'd been relying on her own crutches, instead of seeing her life for what it really was. A dead end that she'd never get past, if she kept slaving away at lousy part-time jobs, or settled for a relationship that had no real chance, no matter how much she wanted it.

"Let's face it," she reasoned. "Under normal circumstances, we never would have hooked up. And as much as I care about Leslie, you and Amanda need to find a way to help her on your own. Just like I need to do something about the mess I've made of my life."

"Leslie needs someone she can talk to, Bailey."

"Then talk to her." She glanced down the hall, then lowered her voice even more. "Or get Amanda to."

"What if *I* need someone to talk to?" Derrick sounded desperate.

And if she stayed now, she'd never be sure if any of that desperation was really for her.

"Then call me sometime, and we'll talk." She'd dreamed as a teenager of being important to him. His kisses as an adult had tempted her to believe that maybe she finally could be. But real emotional commitment was the last thing this man had time for. Which meant she and Derrick finally had something in common. "I'll always be your friend, but I can't…"

"I understand." He was no longer blocking her escape. "I wouldn't want to be part of this scene, either, if I didn't have to."

"Derrick, it's not—"

"Are either one of you planning to tell me what's going on?" Amanda sniped from the dining room.

"I'll see you when I pick Leslie up from the store on Monday." Derrick opened the front door. "Thanks for everything you've done. Let me know what you find out about your boss's missing inventory."

"Derrick." It suddenly felt as if she were abandoning him, rather than walking away from a man who was confusing his need for her help with needing her for himself.

"Don't worry about it," he assured her. "You're off the hook."

He smiled reassuringly as she stepped outside. But his gray eyes were flatter than she'd ever seen them.

Before she could say another word, he'd softly shut the door.

CHAPTER TWELVE

"I'M NOT ASKING YOU, I'm telling you," Spencer Hastings demanded over the phone Thursday evening. "If Capry wants a working dinner tonight, then we meet the man anywhere, anytime he likes. The last thing you want is for the client to think he doesn't have your full attention, and then ask for another lawyer to close the deal."

"Capry *has* my full attention," Derrick said through clenched teeth. He'd pulled into the parking garage a few blocks from Margo's Bistro fifteen minutes ago, and he'd yet to make it out of the car. "I've been working around the clock for Reynolds-Allied, and I'd be happy to meet with the man any other time. But tonight I have a prior commitment."

"Call your date and cancel."

"It's a personal matter with my family."

He was finally joining the group of single parents that Selena sometimes hung out with. A few of the moms were meeting at Margo's tonight, and he had a child at home who'd refused to speak to him since Saturday night. So there he sat, working up the courage to walk two blocks to talk with a table full of strangers, because Selena couldn't make it that night.

His only saving grace was that a call to the bistro had confirmed that Bailey was working the closing shift.

"I don't know what you consider your full attention," Hastings countered, "but your performance this week isn't it. You missed the update you promised the man Monday. You're still playing catch-up after your weekend of family drama. I'm telling you to cancel your plans, and meet us at Masa's at nine."

Hastings hung up, as if further discussion was pointless.

Which it was.

A corporate lawyer's job was to soothe his client's nerves, while he pushed complicated, detail-riddled cases through the courts, and made it all look effortless. A client like Reynolds-Allied, whose business was worth seven figures to the firm this year alone, got whatever one of their executives needed, whenever they needed it.

If Capry wanted to go scuba diving, Derrick was expected to suit up and do the dance.

To make Masa's on time, he'd have to head over

the bridge now, beg his sitter to watch the girls a few hours longer, then shower and change into fresh clothes and head back into San Francisco for a five-star meal he doubted he'd taste.

But what he should be doing was parking his butt at a table in Margo's and asking other single parents what they did when their kids turned on them after their divorces.

And let's not forget your latest chance to stalk Bailey, who clearly doesn't need your problems heaped on top of her own.

Bailey had been friendly and helpful each time he'd picked Leslie up at the store. She was holding her boss at bay about the missing inventory, mostly because nothing else had disappeared in the last week. But she barely looked Derrick in the eye now.

She thought the only reason he'd bothered noticing her was because she was saving him the trouble of dealing with Leslie himself. She didn't trust him any more than his child did.

He pocketed his cell phone and headed for the bistro. Screw drinks and small talk with a client he barely knew.

Tonight was going to be about coffee and small talk with a bunch of women he barely knew. His ex had left in a snit Sunday morning, and it was anyone's guess what Amanda would do next.

He needed to find a way to bond with his daughter.

Now.

No other commitment, even a Reynolds-Allied one, was more important.

"AREN'T YOU WORKING at the bistro tonight?" Beverly asked her granddaughter.

Most nights, Bailey was only home between Stop Right and bistro shifts long enough to say hello, clean up, then leave again. It had been a surprise to find her sitting in the inn's office with the lights off.

"I didn't feel up to it." There were no elbow-deep stacks of files and receipts competing for her attention tonight. Only a single sheet of paper lay on the desk's blotter. "Margo said she'd find someone to cover for me."

"Are you coming down with something?" Beverly flipped on the desk lamp and placed the back of her hand against her granddaughter's forehead. "You're so pale."

Bailey held up the letter she'd been staring at.

"This came from the bank today."

Beverly hesitated, then took it. It wasn't like they hadn't known this moment was coming.

"It's over, isn't it?" She scanned the succinct, professional denial to Bailey's latest request to extend their second mortgage. "We're out of options."

"Well, we can sell, and hopefully make enough for

you to have some kind of retirement. But, yeah. The Gables Inn is done."

"Honey, I'm going to be fine." Beverly made sure she sounded a whole lot more fine than she felt. "I'll get a job if I need a little extra money. Don't—"

"I don't want you to have to get a job!" Her granddaughter slapped her hands to the desk. "I want you to have the house you grew up in. The business you and my father built. I want to go back and find some way to fix this!"

Beverly sat on the edge of the desk, seeing beyond Bailey's panic to the fear that was so unlike her granddaughter.

Or was it?

"There's nothing to fix. There's just the way things are, and I'm going to be okay. *We're* going to be okay, just as soon as you realize that I'm capable of enjoying whatever life I have beyond this place."

Bailey actually smiled at that.

"You're capable of anything you set your mind to, Grams."

"And so are *you*." Beverly swallowed her own panic, and focused on what her granddaughter refused to see. "You're brilliant and work harder than anyone I know. And you gave this place your best shot, every day for eleven years. Now it's time to let go, and figure out what *you* want to do next."

Bailey blinked, her confusion heartbreaking.

"You've never even thought that far, have you?" How could Beverly have not seen that. "All you could see was the fight to save this place, and making me and your father proud. But, honey, your father wanted you to follow your dreams. Now, you'll finally have that chance. Maybe we'll make enough on the sale to get you started doing whatever you want to do next. Maybe even college, though I'm sure you can still find some scholarship money."

"What? No! I don't want your money. I—"

The front desk buzzer intruded. This time of night, it could only mean one of the guests had a problem.

"I've got it." Beverly patted her granddaughter's arm, determined to take care of Bailey for a change. "Try to relax, and I'll bring you a cup of tea, once I deal with whoever's out front."

But when she saw who was waiting in the foyer, it was obvious that this was yet one more problem Bailey would insist on taking care of herself.

WEDDINGS AND SISTER SWITCHES and back-to-school meetings with teachers…

The three women at the cozy bistro table seemed to Derrick to be as close as sisters.

Margo Evans and Nora Clark he'd met once before, the time he'd stopped by hunting for Bailey. It sounded like Nora had not too long ago rolled off a stint at impersonating her twin sister, and she was now engaged to another local—ex-sports personality and skier, Erik Morgan. And all another woman, Rosie DeWitt, could talk about was the local political scene.

The nonstop mom chatter he'd expected was a no-show.

So was Bailey, who'd skipped her shift tonight.

"Derrick, are you enjoying being back in San Francisco after all these years?" Nora asked, all eyes swinging toward him as she spoke. "It must be great to be home."

"Actually, it's been a crazy year. I haven't been able to get out and explore the city much." Not only did he barely know anyone at the table, he barely knew anyone in town. "And it's not like I was here all that long when I was a kid."

"But, Selena said you played football for Western," Margo said.

"Yeah, but we only moved here for my junior and senior years."

"So, you're kind of starting over, figuring out what San Francisco has to offer."

"Sort of." Except he seldom saw the outside of his office building during daylight hours. That kind of put a damper on figuring out much of anything that didn't involve work.

Everyone nodded silently.

Waited for him to say more.

Sipped their coffee.

"I should probably go." He started to stand. Margo's hand covered his, her concerned expression inviting him to sit back down.

"I realize how uncomfortable this must be for you," she said. "But Selena's mentioned how hard you're trying to make things work for you and your girls. Is there something we can do to help?"

"I'm sorry that I barged in on your evening," was his nonresponse. Everyone had been more than friendly, but… "I think this was a bad idea."

"Social coma," Rosie said.

The other women nodded in agreement.

"What?" he asked.

"What you get sucked into," Nora explained. "When you first become a single parent and have to do everything by yourself. It's like the rest of the world has to cease to exist for a while, just so you can survive. Then one day, you poke your head back out of your own problems, and you realize that years have gone by without you even noticing. It's like coming out of some kind of coma."

"You've been drowning alone for so long," Margo agreed, "you forget there's a whole bunch of us out here going through the exact same thing. Once you've been there, you start noticing the signals."

He was giving off signals?

"Don't feel too bad, we've all done it," Rosie

assured him. "Well, everyone but Selena. But she's like Superwoman. Nothing gets to her."

And he was a successful, driven man.

Nothing was supposed to get to him, either.

Except, drowning was exactly the right word. Work, his ex, his girls, the feelings for Bailey he couldn't stop, but had totally bungled… Life had sucked him under, and he was pulling everyone he cared about down with him.

His life sounded like a teaser for the next *Oprah* show.

"If there was a single-parent playbook," Margo said, after several minutes had ticked by, "feeling completely ill-equipped for the job would be the first chapter or section or whatever…."

And that's when it finally struck him, how hard these women were trying to reach him on a *guy* level.

"The first *pattern,*" he chuckled. "Playbooks are all about patterns that you practice over and over again, until you know them by heart. Then when you're in a game, you piece the patterns together into plays, depending on what the other team's doing."

He had everyone's attention, but not the kind of female attention he usually attracted. He wasn't a local celebrity to these women. He was another struggling parent they wanted to get to know and understand, and maybe even help.

He was a friend.

"So, being a single parent is like football?" Now *that*, he could get into.

"You mean like there's one major problem after another hurtling at you, while all you care about is making it down the field?" Nora seemed to be the analytical one of the bunch. She contemplated her analogy, her eyes losing focus for a second. "Sounds about right."

"The touchdowns can be a whole lot of fun, though." Margo's eyes sparkled.

Her latest end zone, according to Selena, had been her surprise wedding last month to her not-so-silent business partner, Robert.

"I like the victory dancing, when you've survived another school year," Rosie chimed in. "Or the first time you manage not to burn breakfast while you pack lunch and finish your boss's latest must-have project, all before the sun comes up. Too bad single parents don't get cheerleaders."

Derrick grunted.

Cheerleaders he could live the rest of his life without.

All he wanted was to make one damn decision that didn't cost the people he cared about more than it helped them.

He sized up the women trying so hard to make him feel welcome, after he'd basically blown their group off for months.

Throw the ball, DC. How many times had his dad

said that, when Derrick first started playing football? *Nothing's ever going to happen for your team, if you're too afraid to throw the ball.*

"So when you've lost the game—" he clenched his hands on top of the table "—and, I mean you've had your ass handed to you, and had to be carried off the field… What do you do then?"

He expected pity when he finally looked up.

Instead, there were more nods of understanding.

Nora even shrugged.

"I usually make myself a cup of hot chocolate," she said. "Get a good night's sleep, and start over the next day."

Not the omniscient answer he'd been hoping for from a table full of experts.

"So what you're saying is…"

"Get used to screwing up." Rosie smiled. "And welcome to the club."

"But—" Derrick's cell phone started vibrating in his pocket.

The name on the display propelled him out of his chair and several feet away from the others as he answered the call.

"Hey," he said. "It's good to hear from you. Listen—"

"Derrick, you need to meet me at your house," Bailey interrupted. "I have Leslie with me."

"What? The sitter was supposed to—"

"The sitter was at your house with Savannah, when I dropped Leslie off on my way home from the Stop Right. Next thing I knew, Leslie showed up at the inn, and I can barely understand what she's saying. She's really upset. Can you get away?"

"Give me fifteen minutes." He was already heading back to the table for his jacket.

He ended the call and pocketed his cell phone.

"Everything okay?" Margo asked.

"No," he said. "Not by a long shot."

CHAPTER THIRTEEN

"I DIDN'T DO IT, DAD," Leslie insisted. "I didn't drink all that stuff."

"Fine, then explain how the empty beer cans missing from the convenience store wound up in our garage," her dad said as he paced across the room and back.

"How do I know?"

Leslie had been working on her science project every afternoon that week, using the workbench in the garage. After getting home from the Stop Right, she'd started messing with the last of the experiments she'd have to reproduce for her teacher, and that's when she noticed that the door was open on her dad's cabinet of abandoned sports equipment.

She'd peeked inside, then she'd bolted out of the garage. And she hadn't stopped running until she'd gotten to Bailey's place. She'd had the crazy notion that the woman would help her. Maybe help Leslie get rid of the stuff, without calling her father.

"I've never even touched that crummy cabinet," she blurted at her dad. "Why would I? And if I was going to hide some empty beer cans I didn't want you to know about, why would I shove them into a pile of your old stuff, then pretend to find them myself?"

"Oh, I don't know." Her dad stopped in front of her. "Maybe because you hate everything about your life here, and you don't want a day to go by without reminding me that it's all my fault. So you made sure I wouldn't miss the result of your latest temper tantrum."

"Like you're ever home long enough to find anything I might have stashed here."

"I searched the place top to bottom last week!" He shook his head slightly, then inhaled for round two. "I want to trust you, Leslie. But what am I supposed to think? What was it? I didn't find the beer fast enough, so you ran to Bailey and upped the ante?"

"I didn't! Bailey, you believe me, don't you?" On the ride over, the woman had listened quietly to Leslie's story. At least the part of it Leslie had calmed down enough to get out. And Bailey had just as quietly been watching the last five minutes of Cavenaugh family therapy, after the sitter had headed home. "I wouldn't—"

"I believe you." Bailey shook her head at Leslie's dad, the same way Selena did sometimes when she thought he was being a bonehead. "But it *is* the same brand of beer that's missing from the store. The same amount."

"Then someone else drank it and put it there."

When Leslie got her hands on Ginger, she was going to kill her.

"Who would do something like that?" her dad asked. "Why would they even bother?"

"What do you care? You had to leave another all-nighter at work. That's what you're steamed about."

"I wasn't at work. And what I *care* about is you getting yourself into something I won't be able to help you get out of. Shoplifting, condoms, drugs, now drinking. What's next?"

"I didn't do it! I wouldn't make that kind of trouble for Bailey."

"But making trouble for me is just fine, is that it?"

"You said it, not me." She headed for her bedroom, knowing her dad wouldn't follow.

God forbid that he *really* wanted to talk with her about anything.

"IF YOU'LL COVER THE EXPENSE," Bailey offered, "I'll replace the beer and the wine coolers at the store, and tell Drayton I found them buried in the storeroom."

If she didn't leave now, she was going to lose what was left of her temper.

"Wait." Derrick grabbed her arm, letting go only when she stopped trying to yank away. "What's wrong?"

"You just told your daughter you think she's capable of stealing again and underage drinking, after Leslie went out of her way to own up to what she found."

"To you! Whenever she has a crisis now, and she needs to talk to someone about it, she turns to you."

"And that's whose fault, exactly? You asked me to get to know Leslie, to maybe be someone your daughter thinks she can trust. And now that I am, you're jealous?"

Meanwhile, she'd been talking herself out of calling him all afternoon, ever since she'd opened the "rest in peace" letter from the bank. The weak part of her that had needed to lean on someone, just for a few minutes, had gone on to picture her resting her head on Derrick's shoulder, until the world righted itself again.

Clearly, she'd had a moment of temporary insanity.

"Jealous of you?" He stepped closer, his eyes alive with more than just anger now. "I'm blown away. Ashamed. I just spent an hour with Selena's single-parent friends, trying to get some clue about how to talk to my own children. And Leslie ran all the way to the inn to tell you her latest secret. She could have called me on my cell, or waited until I got home. But she wanted to talk to you. How do you do it? How can you be exactly what we need, when we've only known you for a few weeks?"

Bailey's own anger turned into confusion so quickly, she reached a hand toward a nearby chair to keep her balance. She found herself caught, instead, against the firm wall of Derrick's chest, one of his arms around her waist, the fingers of the other hand freeing her ponytail and then threading through her hair.

"Thank you," he said, when all she could manage was to stare at the curves of his lips. "For helping my daughter when she won't even sit in the same room with me."

He was staring, too, his mouth lowering for a kiss that would only complicate things more. She ducked her head, and his lips grazed her cheek.

They hadn't spoken all week, until Leslie showed up on her doorstep. Bailey couldn't afford to forget that.

"You… You were with Selena's friends at Margo's tonight?"

He nodded, his forehead resting against hers until he straightened.

"I blew off an important business dinner to sit at a table full of women I don't know, and look so obviously clueless that everyone there had me pegged in under an hour."

"That's great. I'm…I'm proud of you, Derrick." She had to let go, or she'd never be able to leave. "But you should be in there talking with Leslie now, not—"

"I know. I have to keep trying to get through to her, no matter how many times I fail. I get that now. I've *been* trying, every night since Amanda left. And I'm not going to give up. But what if Leslie's never able to trust me? What if she never forgets that I haven't been there for her all these years?"

"You're here now." Bailey couldn't stop herself from laying a hand over his heart. "You have to make her understand that you'd do anything to earn her trust back."

The lure of wanting him to tell her the exact same thing was making it impossible for Bailey to walk away.

"Stay." He pulled her closer, until every inch of her was pressed against expensively clad muscle.

"For...for Leslie?" She really needed to get back to Grams, and he really needed to believe he could deal with his daughter on his own.

"For me." His hand trailed down her spine, pressing at the curve of her lower back. "Even though it was another emergency with Leslie, hearing your voice on the other end of the phone made my day. My week. I wasn't just racing home to my daughter, Bailey. I couldn't wait to get here and see you again, regardless of the circumstances. Stay for me."

"Are you sure?"

He had to be sure.

They both did.

"I'm sure that I need you in my life even more than Leslie does. You have to believe that, no matter how many messed-up signals I'm sending you right now. Because even though I've only had a few weeks to get to know you, I can't remember what it's like not to want you. I can't stop kicking myself for being too stupid to notice you when we were in school."

"I was just a kid."

"You're magnificent, now and then. If you could help Savannah get ready for bed... If you don't have anything else going on tonight..."

"I...I guess it could wait until morning," Bailey heard herself saying. Grams and the postmortem of their family business weren't going anywhere. "In fact, some time in the next few days, Grams and I could really use some legal advice."

His eyebrows drew together.

"What's wrong?"

She shook her head, her smile almost effortless, because for the first time in years, there was no point in obsessing about what was going to happen tomorrow. Tomorrow was finally a given, at least until it was time to follow those dreams Grams kept insisting Bailey still had.

Tonight was all that she had to worry about right now.

And tonight Derrick Cavenaugh was holding her in his arms and saying he needed her.

"Go talk with Leslie. I'll be here when you're through."

I DON'T WANT TO TALK anymore tonight, Dad.

Leslie had sounded so exhausted.

Derrick hadn't had the heart to keep her up a minute longer, even if he could have sat there forever and listened to his daughter finally spilling her guts about everything. The troublemaker she'd befriended, who'd taken the booze from the store instead of Leslie. The nonexistent boys she'd been threatening to do way too much with, when she still hadn't kissed anyone yet.

But at some point over the last hour, he'd heard Savannah head to bed, and both girls had school in the morning.

And Bailey had said she'd wait for him.

Softly shutting his daughter's door, he ran a hand down his wrinkled suit and headed for the den. The tempting aroma of coffee lured him toward the kitchen.

Bailey was standing at the counter. A tiny, fiery dynamo who'd dropped everything for his child—again—but who'd stayed this time for him. She turned when he walked in, questions in her eyes that he didn't want to hear.

He couldn't let her think this moment was about Leslie.

"I thought you could use this." She held out a mug of coffee.

He took it, only to set it aside. A stimulant was the last thing he needed with a woman like Bailey in the room. He stepped closer and took her mug, too, placing it beside his.

"Savannah's tucked in for the night." Her pulse fluttered at the base of her throat.

He could feel every beat of his own.

No other woman had called to him like Bailey, with her intelligence and determination to take care of everyone, her rich coloring, combined with how simply she dressed, as if she had no idea how truly beautiful she was.

Maybe she had been a distraction at first. Another easy excuse to avoid owning up to his responsibilities as a single father. But Bailey had pushed him every step of the way. Challenged him to stand on his own.

And tonight he had.

He couldn't think of anyone he'd rather celebrate that milestone with.

"Leslie was already half-asleep when we finished up." He brushed a palm down Bailey's side, until his hand was covering the soft cotton that dipped in at her tiny waist. "I like your T-shirts."

"Why?" She looked down at the plain men's shirt she'd probably bought in a pack of three.

"Because they make me wonder what you'd look like in one of mine." He couldn't help it. His hand had already found the hem. Not touching the quivering skin beneath wasn't any more of an option than not kissing those lips that parted as she gasped. "Or whether you're even softer underneath."

He captured her mouth, bracing his free hand

against the counter beside her hip. On the football field and in the boardroom, he was known for his patience. His willingness to wait for the right play, the right option, before making his move.

But all his brain could manage with Bailey Greenwood in his arms, was, *now!*

Bailey's mouth broke free, but her hands were running up his chest, sending every muscle she caressed into a spasm that ricocheted straight to the neediest part of him.

"What about Leslie?" she asked. "The beer, and—"

"Later." He palmed her firm bottom. Swallowed her groan. Set her on the counter, so he could press between her thighs. "Tomorrow."

Her hands framed his face, green eyes glittering with unshed tears, reminding him of the finest jewels.

"Derrick." She avoided his mouth when he would have kissed her again. "I could want you more than I've ever wanted anything in my life. But not if this is just about you needing to feel something good tonight. I'm too desperate for that myself right now. Desperate enough to make a really bad decision, if we're not careful."

He took her wrists in his hands, circling their fragile strength with fingers he realized were shaking.

Hearing how much he could mean to her was more powerful than the need pulsing through him.

"I was certain I couldn't ever want anything the way

I wanted to play pro ball," he said. "Now, I'd give everything good I've ever had to see my girls happy. And to have you be a part of that, any way you want to be."

The sparkle dimmed in her eyes as Bailey lowered her hands. "Of course your girls deserve to be happy, and I'll do anything I can for Leslie."

She tried to slip off the counter.

He held tight.

"That's not what I meant." *Way to fumble in the end zone, DC.* "I'm not looking for an ace babysitter, or someone to keep Leslie and Savannah's minds off their messed-up parents. You deserve to be happy, too, Bailey. I want the chance to give you everything you've always dreamed of. I want a part of that to be me."

"I—" she was shaking her head "—I'm not sure… It's been a long time since I've even thought about what I want. And now, the last few days… I don't know…."

"Then don't think. Just let yourself trust me. I'm not looking for an easy way out of dealing with my problems. As great as you are with Leslie, that's not what I want. Not tonight. I want whatever this is I'm feeling every time we're together. And I want to stop looking over my shoulder when you're not here, wondering when I'll see you again. If you're ever coming back to me."

He stole whatever she tried to say next, kissing her softly, feeding off her sweetness.

"Don't be afraid of me, Bailey. Stop trying to find

reasons to push me away." He kissed her fingers, then let her go. "I won't pressure you into anything you're not sure about. I don't want this to be one more thing I mess up, because I don't know how to stop pushing when it comes to having things my way. But, I can't stop thinking about you, I can't stop needing…"

"Something to feel like winning again?" she finished for him.

It was on the tip of his tongue to demand to know everything she thought she'd lost, so he could find a way to get it all back for her. But then she was filling his arms again, leaning into him, searching for his mouth with her own, needing and wanting and craving as fiercely as he did.

He kissed a path down her neck, biting into soft flesh as he lifted her trembling body off the counter and into his arms. Her legs wrapped around his waist as he walked from the kitchen to the den. When he laid her on the couch, she squeaked in surprise, then sighed as his body pressed her into the cushions.

He needed—he wanted—to cherish and devour her, all at the same time.

Rein it in, DC.

Keep it cool.

But when he caressed her, she arched her hips. His hands whispered beneath her shirt again, and hers pulled him even closer.

"Derrick, I need—"

"I know, honey." The power of her need rolled off her, fueling the demands his own body was making. "Touch me. Show me. Anything."

The delicate clasp of her bra came apart in his hands. His dress shirt met the same fate, except she tore at the fabric, several buttons clattering to the hardwood floor beneath the couch. Her softness burned his fingers. Her nails bit into his flesh. Their mouths ate at one another, their teeth nipping, their tongues tasting. They shared a groan as their hands stalled, the backs of their fingers touching, their breath churning.

"The girls…" he managed to whisper, his eyes feasting on the sight of her nipples peaking against the T-shirt he wanted to rip away from her body and keep forever.

"I know." Her touch stalled at his waist.

He took her hands in his again, and grimaced at the effort it took to push back until they were sitting side-by-side.

"We…" He cleared the roughness from his voice. "Savannah or Leslie could—"

"Wander out here any minute." Bailey laid her head against his shoulder, as if she'd been doing it forever. "We can't do this."

"We sure as hell can." He tipped her chin up. "Just not like this. Not tonight."

"I should—" She stalled as his thumb pressed against her mouth.

She was probably back to telling herself to leave, before things went too far.

Didn't she realize? They'd gone too far the second she'd told him she wanted this as much as he did.

"No, you shouldn't." A chaste kiss shouldn't smolder, but he could feel steam rising from the one he gave her next. "We're not going to take this any further right now, but that doesn't mean you don't belong here."

She glanced away, then turned her head until her face was hidden against his neck.

"What am I doing here?" The vibration of her voice against his skin was hell on his good intentions. "I... You..."

"I'm the luckiest bastard to ever graduate from Western High," he insisted. "I've gotten to see what I've been missing all these years, and I'm getting the chance to start all over again, and do things right this time."

Kissing the soft hair curling on top of her head, he smoothed his hand down the length of it, until he was rubbing her back. His fingers tingled from even that casual a touch.

"What's going on with you and your grandmother?" he asked, grabbing hold of the first safe topic that came to mind. "You said you needed legal advice?"

Bailey lifted her head away, and calmly disengaged their bodies.

Too calmly.

"What's wrong?" he asked, once she'd settled

against the corner of the couch, a throw pillow clutched in her lap.

She shrugged.

"No big deal. We need to find a buyer for the inn, that's all."

He tugged her arm until she let him pull her back.

No big deal.

"I knew things were getting tight, but what happened?"

"I blew it, that's what happened!" She leaned more heavily against him this time, her misery a living thing. "We have no money, and the IRS isn't interested in our sob story. They want what they're due, so we've got to find someone who'll fork up the cash."

"What about the bank? I saw your grandmother there the other day—"

"Not going to happen. I've dipped into that well one too many times."

"But—"

"No!" she insisted. "There's no *but.* I've been fighting off the *buts* long enough to know what I'm talking about. I've scrimped and scraped and done promotion on the cheap and combined special offerings with other local businesses and danced around the truth for years. It's time to face facts. I'm not the business prodigy everyone thought I was. I don't have the first clue what I'm doing. Brains aren't worth a damn if you can't put them to work when you

need them. And clearly, I can't. It took my grandmother too long to figure that out, and now she's
going to lose her home because of it."

"She's not blaming you for this?"

"Of course not." And it sounded like that made everything worse.

"Then why are you flogging yourself? Seventy-
five percent of all small businesses fail. I should
know. My firm makes a living helping corporations
gobble up what's left, after an entrepreneur can't
quite turn a great idea into gold."

It was one of the parts of his job that he liked the
least, but a very real fact of the business world.

"I know." Bailey agreed. "And being a statistic
might be comforting, if it weren't my grandmother's
future and her past that I've destroyed."

"You haven't—"

"That house is her family. Her history. It's what
she wanted to pass on to my father and then to me
and maybe one day to my kids. Now, she's going to
have to say goodbye to all of it, and watch someone
else do whatever they want with the place. And I
don't care how hard anyone tries to convince me that
that's okay, or that it's not my fault. I promised her
I would handle it, and I didn't."

"So if she'd brought in another business manager,
then the Bay area's tourist economy would miracu-
lously have revamped itself in your favor?" Bailey

knew better than that. "You're a suburban bed and breakfast competing against luxury, boutique hotels popping up all over the city. If you'd had more capital, maybe a third-party financial backer, it would have leveled the playing field. But—"

"Grams never wanted a partner," Bailey admitted. "She liked the inn quaint and small-town. The investors who've shown interest wanted to upgrade and modernize things that she liked the way they were."

"From what I've seen of the place, I can understand why."

"She always said she'd rather take her chances and keep things the way they've always been, than turn her home into something she wouldn't want to stay in herself."

"So that's what you did."

"Yes."

"Even though you knew it was a risk."

"Doing anything else would have made Grams miserable."

Bailey's shoulders rose and fell.

"Then it sounds to me like you took care of your grandmother first, then you did everything you could to make the business work the way she wanted it to. If that means you're not ready for the cutthroat world of corporate business, then thank God. Who needs another shark trolling the waters? You put your heart out there every day, caring about how your decisions affected the person you were helping. That doesn't make you a failure, Bailey. It makes you amazing."

He kissed her temple, taking her silence as an encouraging sign. She'd said she needed his help. And it sounded as if what she needed most was someone to reason stuff through with, until she could see things more clearly.

"So, you want to talk about it some more?" he finally asked, certain he'd never uttered that particular phrase to a woman before.

"Really?" Her tone reeked of skepticism.

"Unless you've got any better ideas for passing the time."

He settled against the back of the couch and cuddled her closer. His hand just happened to brush the underside of her breast in the process, but what was a guy to do.

"Stop that!" She swatted his arm.

"Then start talking. I'm not ready to let you go yet, and we're fresh out of nongroping options to occupy our time. Unless you want to dig out one of Savannah's favorite board games, and go at that one-on-one."

The woman looked too damn sexy, the way she flushed at whatever one-on-one image had flashed through her mind.

Derrick anchored her back firmly to his chest and nestled her head under his chin. Then he waited for her muscles to relax.

"Talking, it is," he said. "So, let's have it. Tell me how you single-handedly set out to ruin your grandmother's life."

She chuckled as she began this time, instead of sounding like she was about to cry.

Then something startling happened. Caught up in the sound of her voice, in the feel of her leaning so trustingly into him, he found himself relaxing, too.

He checked his watch and realized that if Spencer had had his way, Derrick would still be downtown, brandishing an expensive bottle of wine to medicate an important client's anxiety attack—instead of home, where his daughter needed him, holding the closest thing to perfection he'd ever had in his arms.

CHAPTER FOURTEEN

"LES, GET UP," Savannah demanded. She pulled on Leslie's covers, then yanked away the pillow Leslie was using to block out the high-voltage beam of the bedside lamp the kid had switched on. "Leslie, we're going to be late for school, and Dad's not in his room. Get up!"

Peeling one eyelid open, Leslie saw enough of the blurry numbers on her radio alarm clock to know they weren't anywhere near Def Con 1.

"We've got almost an hour before the bus gets here."

"But Dad never lets us sleep this late."

The radio went off.

Leslie slapped the snooze button and rolled back over.

Rushing to school, today of all days, made as much sense as running into a blazing fire because she needed a tan.

She was going to have it out with Ginger. She was going to make sure that nothing else was stolen at the Stop Right, and no more surprises were left lying around to upset her family. Her dad had finally found a way to trust her. He'd followed her into her room last night, and he hadn't left until they'd talked through everything.

No way was Leslie letting Ginger mess any of that up.

But being in a hurry to confront her former partner in crime was a totally different story.

"Leslie," Savannah whined.

"I'll be up in a few minutes." Like, maybe thirty or so. "Dad's probably in the kitchen trying not to burn breakfast."

"He's not here." Savannah pulled the pillow away again, this time tossing it across the room, where it landed with a soft thud. The early-morning silence of the house finally registered. "No one's here. And his bed looks like he didn't sleep in it last night."

"Of course he's here." Leslie scurried toward the door. Her dad had come right out and said he loved her last night, over and over again. That he'd do whatever it took to make her believe that. "He wouldn't just leave."

She rushed to his room, Savannah in tow. Then she made a beeline for the deserted den. There was no one there, no sound, except for the grandfather clock ticking away in the corner. Her eyes stung as she turned to head for the kitchen. Her heart felt like it was shrinking with each step.

Then a soft snore from the direction of the couch

caused her to turn back at the same moment that something moved on the cushions.

Shrieking, she put a hand over her mouth. The two people who'd been curled up together sprung apart. Savannah rushed to her side, her eyes round as saucers.

"What!" her dad asked, running a hand over his eyes and through his hair, then checking his watch. "Oh, damn."

"Oh, no." Bailey glanced from Leslie to her dad, then back. "I can't believe we fell asleep."

"You've been here all night?" Leslie asked. "Are you guys—"

"We were talking." Her dad stood. He looked ridiculous tucking in his wrinkled shirt, as if that would erase all of Leslie's questions about why the thing had been pulled loose in the first place. And why there were no buttons left for him to button. "It was late, and I was helping Bailey work through a few things, and—"

"I guess we fell asleep," Bailey finished.

Half lying on top of each other?

Leslie nodded.

She was smiling, actually, and she wasn't even sure why.

She gave her sister's shoulder a nudge.

"See, I told you Dad was here. You dragged me out of bed for nothing."

"Why didn't you sleep in your own room,

Daddy?" the clueless wonder asked. "Why did you make Bailey sleep out here, when we have an extra room next to mine?"

"Bailey and I didn't mean to fall asleep." He gave up on the shirt, both hands landing on his hips. "You two get ready for school, and I'll find us something to eat."

Savannah dragged her feet as she headed back down the hall, delaying her retreat.

No way was Leslie giving up her ringside seat.

"You, too." Her dad motioned over his shoulder with his thumb. He took Bailey's hand in his. "Give us a few minutes to—"

The doorbell rang, and all three of them jumped again.

"I'll get it," Leslie finally said.

Both adults began smoothing at their messed-up clothes some more.

Another ring came before she reached the door.

"Hold your horses." She flipped the lock and turned the knob.

"Oh, God," she said, the instant she saw who was on the other side.

"HOW COULD YOU LET that woman sleep over, with my daughters right down the hall!" Amanda demanded.

Bailey glanced toward the bedrooms where both Cavenaugh girls were getting ready for school.

"We didn't mean for it to—" Derrick began.

"All this time," Amanda ranted on, "you've been treating me like a leper for moving on after our divorce and remarrying. I'm the bad parent, for wanting to be happy. You've taken my children across the country to keep them away from me. And now I find out it's because you wanted me out of the way, so you could keep chasing every cheap skirt that crosses your path, without me questioning what kind of example you're setting for my girls! No wonder you didn't want me to stay here last weekend. Were you sleeping with her then?"

"Bailey and I didn't sleep together last night," Derrick insisted, while Bailey grappled for a nonconfrontational reply to the "cheap skirt" remark.

"Right!" Amanda's gaze catalogued their clothing.

"Not the way you're implying," Bailey finally managed.

The other woman stepped to the couch and dug Bailey's bra out from between the cushions. She twirled it around one finger.

"You were just talking all night, is that it?"

Derrick yanked the lingerie from his ex and handed it to Bailey.

"Knock it off, Amanda." He dug his hands into his pockets. "I'm allowed to do whatever I damn well please in the privacy of my own home. Bailey and I don't have to explain ourselves to you or anyone else, except to say that we were responsible and went out of our way to do nothing that would have confused or upset the girls."

"And I'm supposed to believe you, after what I just walked in on? The mighty Derrick Cavenaugh had a woman's bra off, and I have no doubt the little tramp was crawling all over you. They always do," she added for Bailey's benefit, before refocusing her glare on her ex. "But you were a Boy Scout, is that it? Do you really expect me to believe you didn't lap up every last scrap this little nobody threw at you?"

The pettiness of the other woman's jealousy wasn't the worst part. The picture Amanda painted of Derrick being chased, and caught, by other women over the years, maybe even when he was still married, washed through Bailey like a wave of frigid water.

She looked down at her shapeless clothes, then at Amanda's designer ensemble, understanding in that instant that if she was a nobody, it was her own doing. She'd gone out of her way to play the part of a nobody with no future. No dreams. No chance for more than she already had.

Then the *more* she'd always wanted had walked back into her life, and she had no clue what to do with either him or herself.

"I need to get to work." A glamorous morning shift at the Stop Right beckoned.

Derrick threaded his fingers through hers and

squeezed. His worried gaze read the hurt she couldn't hide.

"Actually, Bailey's the one who stopped things last night." He lifted her hand to his lips and kissed the backs of her fingers, his eyes only for her. "We've agreed to take things slow, until the timing is better."

"Yes," Amanda sniped. "I can see that."

"Not that it's any of your business—" Derrick finally looked toward his ex "—but I can understand how this must look. Let me make things as clear as I can, so we can dispense with the drama and move on to what the hell you're doing here at the crack of dawn. I'm interested in Bailey, yes. But I haven't been chasing skirts all over San Francisco, any more than I chased them in Atlanta. In fact, I haven't slept with anyone but you since our wedding night. I can honestly say that until Bailey, being with another woman was the last thing on earth I wanted, after finally getting you out of my life."

Bailey's shocked gasp echoed Amanda's.

But while the other woman's hand raised to her throat at Derrick's description of just how much he'd wanted to be rid of her, Bailey struggled with the reality of being the first woman who'd tempted mighty Derrick Cavenaugh in years.

She fought the panicked need to go back to being a nobody, who could slink off to her nowhere job and enjoy her obscurity.

"Why are you here, Amanda?" Derrick hugged Bailey to his side. "We're already running late."

"To help with Leslie, of course." Righteous indignation cozied up against the bitterness in the death glare the woman shot at Bailey. "My daughter needs me. And I'm staying this time, until we figure out what's best for my child."

"AMANDA'S TAKING the girls for the weekend?" Selena's hand stalled in the process of handing over money to pay for the chips and soda she'd brought to the counter.

She'd stopped by the Stop Right on the way to meet with a Langston client—and to snoop out an update on last night's drama, after Derrick raced away from her friends at the bistro. And Bailey, in the midst of the longest shift of her life, hadn't been able to resist venting and filling her new friend in on the latest.

"The girls will be staying with her in the city, at the Monticello." Anywhere but the den of iniquity Bailey had evidently turned Derrick's place into. "Amanda said she was so disturbed by what she learned about Leslie last weekend, she's stepping in to clean up Derrick's mess. Savannah's nonstop talking about everything she wants to do in the city with her mom. Leslie looks like she's prepping for World War Three."

Selena let loose a shrill whistle.

"Sounds to me like the honeymoon's over." She twisted off the soda's cap and took a long drink.

"What honeymoon?"

"Amanda's." The artist smiled at Bailey's mystified expression. "Guess you don't have time to keep up with the sports report. The woman's football-star husband is on the road the next few weekends, playing away games, and then pimping for one of his sponsors. Top media markets, with five-star functions beckoning at every stop. Exactly the sort of limelight that Amanda eats up. Except suddenly she's back here instead? Makes you wonder."

"Her daughter's in crisis."

"Her daughter's been in crisis for over a year, but Amanda's new guy isn't really a kid kind of person. Obviously, it was best for everyone, if the girls weren't underfoot while things played themselves out."

"Unless the kids weren't the real problem to begin with," Bailey reasoned.

"You mean maybe Ms. Thing's been using them as a scapegoat to hide whatever else isn't working with her second marriage?"

"Or maybe they're an excuse now for getting closer to Derrick again," Bailey said before she could stop herself. "That is—"

"I know exactly what you mean." Selena chuckled. "But I don't think you have anything to worry about."

"I'm not worried." Bailey dug the woman's

change out of the register and handed it over. "Except for what all this will do to the girls. Leslie's just starting to settle down. She's starting to trust Derrick a little more. She's actually talking to him, and—"

"Getting used to the idea of you maybe being in his life?"

"I'm *not* in Derrick's anything."

But how much Bailey wanted to believe she one day might be was terrifying. After all her nagging, telling Derrick he needed to be more emotionally available to his children, Bailey was the one increasingly ready to run from whatever was growing between them.

"You're *in* enough for him to ask you to spend the night."

"It wasn't like that. If Amanda thinks anything serious happened, she misunderstood."

"Yeah, but she's not stupid. Whatever she walked in on this morning may have been platonic, but Amanda's been reading between the lines since we were in high school. She knows what a woman in love looks like. Especially when that woman's in love with a man Amanda still feels proprietary about."

"But I'm not…" The denial wouldn't come, no matter how badly she needed to say it.

"Of course you are." Selena reached across the counter and squeezed her fingers. "If I don't miss my guess, Derrick's head over heels himself. I'm thrilled.

But don't think for a second that Amanda will be. And given the way that Leslie's attached to you, and—"

"You're being overly dramatic. I'm—"

"You're the reason Derrick's smiling again, for the first time since moving back here. Probably for a lot longer than that. You're the key to him believing he can get through to his daughter. The reason he doesn't give a damn what Amanda does anymore, and that's got to be driving her crazy."

"Even if she wants him back, the woman can't honestly see me as competition."

Serena squinted an artist's eye as she tilted her head first one way, then the other, looking Bailey over.

"I think Amanda doesn't have a chance." She winked. "And neither does Derrick, if you ever decide to let him try to convince you he's serious."

"I'll have to convince myself I'm serious first." Bailey looked down at the don't-look-at-me ensemble she'd been hiding in for years.

"Let me know when you decide to give it a shot, 'cause that's something I'd pay money to see." Selena's playfulness vanished as Bailey shook her head. "Come on. Those eyes, that hair. Your teeny-tiny frame that looks better in men's clothes than my hips will ever look in a ball gown. You're a natural. Always were, even in high school, when I caught you drooling over Derrick from across calculus class.

And then caught Amanda scowling at you while you were doing it."

"I didn't…" Bailey stopped mentally thumbing through her hopeless wardrobe of jeans and T-shirts. "Amanda didn't—"

"You both absolutely did. And there the Mighty DC was, oblivious to all of it. Emotions never were his strong suit. Neither was paying attention to anything that wasn't his top priority. So you can see why both Amanda and I would find it significant that he'd be satisfied hanging out with you last night, instead of working his butt off on that merger deal of his."

"IT'S GOOD TO FINALLY SEE you at your desk," Spencer Hastings said. "But Margery tells me you've been working on a new case. With the merger pending—"

"It's just a little research." Derrick hadn't had to look far into the firm's records on Premier Spa, or the local real estate market, to know that Premier's starting offer for the Gables Inn had been a bargain-basement attempt to pad their balance sheet. "I'll only be a few more minutes—"

"You don't have a few minutes for anything but Reynolds-Allied, is that clear?" Hastings rested his hands on the edge of Derrick's desk. "Especially after last night."

"What about last night?" That morning's events left room for remembering little else.

The stolen merchandise Bailey said she'd be replacing at the Stop Right.

Amanda's ultimatum about having the girls to herself for the weekend.

Waking with Bailey in his arms.

"You never showed at Masa's. Capry's talking about wanting me to take over the final phase of the merger. Having you fly second chair for the rest of the deal."

Derrick's gaze lifted from the computer screen.

"There wouldn't *be* a merger if it weren't for the eighteen hours a day I've put in for the last year. You brought me into the firm to handle this project, and it's handled. Dinner doesn't mean shi—"

"It means the client wants your undivided attention." Spencer pushed away from the desk. "And in this case, he doesn't have it. This is the big time, Derrick. I hired you for your image first, then your degree. I could have had a hundred other lawyers with your kind of brains, but your football legacy set you apart. It gets attention. You're a winner, and this firm looks like a winner because we have you. Make the mistake of turning quality-of-life on me, and all that will change, take my word for it."

"Quality of life?" Derrick stood, towering over the other man. "I'm a father, and my child ran crying to someone else last night, because I haven't been there for her in years. Because I've been busting my hump here for you, or for my firm back in Atlanta.

And that's fine. My choice. But there are limits to what I'm willing to sacrifice for this job, Spencer. And my daughters' happiness comes first. If I don't fix things with Leslie, I'll lose her. If I don't figure out how to be a hands-on parent *while* I take care of my career, my relationship with Savannah will be the next casualty."

As would his relationship with Bailey.

He glanced at the Premier Spa financials he'd been reviewing, and clicked his mouse to print.

"So you're telling me you're fine with losing the lead on this account?" Spencer, who'd pretty much ignored his own wife and kids for the better part of twenty years, was understandably mystified. "What about the junior partner position you said you wanted?"

"Oh, I still want it." But Derrick wanted a life he could live with, one that his kids could live with, more. "My commitment to my work hasn't changed. I'll do the job you hired me to do. But being at your beck and call, pandering to clients at a moment's notice, will have to take a backseat sometimes. If I have a pressing personal issue that needs to be taken care of, those are the kinds of *meetings* you can handle yourself from now on."

"I DON'T KNOW WHAT you've done with the rest of the stuff you took." Leslie had cornered Ginger in the hallway outside of geometry class, then had all but dragged her into the bathroom. "And I think Bailey's got me covered at the store, so I don't care what you do with it. But don't ever come to my house again. Don't think you can make trouble for me there. I've told my dad everything, and if you don't back off, he's going to call your mother."

"Not if he doesn't want to bust up your deal with that nasty man who owns the Stop Right. Your dad can't rat on me, without sending you straight to the judge."

"And I told him that's what I wanted him to do, if it means getting you off my back."

"You what!" Ginger stopped fluffing her hair.

"I told my father everything." Something Leslie had never been able to say before. "And he's not going to rat out anyone, as long as you back off. But I've messed up things for him and Bailey enough. I never should have let you in the storeroom. I should have told someone about what you took, as soon as I realized what you and Brett did."

"Yeah, then I would have kicked your butt."

"You wanna kick it now?" Leslie stood straighter, no longer slumping her shoulders to make it harder to tell that she was several inches taller than the other girls her age. It was kinda cool, the way Ginger backed up a couple of feet. "Go ahead. Give it a try."

"You're nuts." Ginger headed for the door.

Leslie grabbed her arm, capturing a slither of bright red hair between her fingers.

"No. I'm done caring what you think about me. I'm over wanting to trash my life the way you do yours."

"Let me go!" Ginger yanked away. She rubbed at the sore spot on her scalp.

"Gladly. Just stay away from me and my family. I'll take you down, if you don't. Whatever trouble that causes me will be worth the satisfaction."

"Like I give a shit about you, you psycho!" Ginger checked her overdone makeup in the hazy mirror above one of the chipped sinks.

Leslie left Ginger to her pursuit of being knocked up or kicked out of school, or both, by the time she was fifteen. A ride Leslie had come way too close to taking herself.

But her dad had stuck by her. He hadn't given up. He'd made the time to get to know her, instead, at least enough to trust her again. Now if they could just get her mom back on the other side of the country where she belonged, they just might have a chance to see what came next.

CHAPTER FIFTEEN

"I THINK YOU HAVE THE CHANCE to make a nice deal for yourself." Derrick forked down another piece of coconut pie, while Bailey and her grandmother finished reviewing the list of local real estate attorneys he'd brought by. "My advice would be for you to work with a lawyer independent of the firm your prospective buyer's using. That way, you're assured you have someone looking out for your best interests."

And damn it if independent didn't have a nice ring to it, after Derrick's ball-busting conversation with Hastings that morning.

"But—" Beverly Greenwood pushed her own plate away, her pie untouched. "Isn't Premier Spa represented by—"

"Hastings Chase Whitney?" Derrick used a starched linen napkin to wipe pie crust from the corner of his mouth. "Yes, ma'am. So naturally, as an attorney for the firm, I'm not at liberty to discuss anything about their offer without their consent."

"But you can bring us a list of your competitors?" Bailey asked. "Whom you think we need to consider working with before we accept any offers."

"Just being neighborly."

Not exactly the word for what had been on his mind ever since Amanda came by the house and picked up the girls for the weekend. But Beverly Greenwood *had* said the inn's door was always open to neighbors. So he'd let himself in, and he wasn't leaving until Bailey agreed to spend the next two days—and nights—with him.

"You'll need your own lawyer," he advised, "if you're still thinking about selling."

Mrs. Greenwood covered her granddaughter's hand. "We don't have much of a choice."

"And from the sound of it, you'll need to close on the sale relatively quickly." Premier's ridiculous starting offer flashed through his mind.

"Bailey thinks she can delay the IRS for a while longer, if we can prove to them that we're making arrangements to pay. But the longer we wait, the more interest they'll pile on."

"The time constraint puts you at a disadvantage any corporate attorney worth his fee wouldn't think twice about exploiting." If it were his deal, Derrick certainly wouldn't. "You'll be prey to whatever half-baked offer comes along first, unless you have a shark of your own making sure you get a fair shake."

"And you don't think *fair* is what Premier has in mind?" Bailey's eyes were warmer than he'd ever seen them.

"I couldn't say."

"But another lawyer from another firm could." Mrs. Greenwood was smiling now.

He concentrated on his last bite of pie, then finished the ice-cold milk that had come with it. "You're a wonderful cook, Mrs. Greenwood."

"Thank you, young man. Baking has become one of my favorite pastimes. I've actually been thinking about doing a little more of it. Maybe catering to a few of the area businesses that might want pastries for their employees' breakfasts. Maybe some local restaurants that want to add gourmet items to their menus."

"Since when?" Bailey blinked in surprise.

"Since it started looking like we might not make it here. It's just an idea I've been tossing around. It might be time to see if I can really do it. Of course I'd need an industrial kitchen wherever I live next, and whether or not I could afford that would depend on—"

"How good a deal we get for the Gables." Bailey looked down at the list of attorneys, then at Derrick.

"I hear that Mike Grantham is always looking for new clients," he said. "He has a good rep for negotiating with corporate buyers."

"Friend of yours?" Bailey had been running her finger down the list. It returned to Grantham's name, right where Derrick had typed it—at the top.

"Never met the man." Derrick shrugged. "But I understand he's made quite a bit of trouble for the firm over the years."

"Is giving us this information going to make trouble for *you* at work?" Bailey asked.

"It's not a breech of ethics. Not technically. And you're entitled to engage any legal counsel you choose to handle your sale."

"But…" Beverly Greenwood frowned. "If you're putting your job at risk…"

"Don't worry about it." Derrick wasn't. "Coming here was my decision. It's important that you're protected. And at least in the case of Premier Spa, I can't take care of that for you, no matter how much I'd like to. All I've told you is that Grantham's the best independent out there. What you do with that information is up to you."

"I don't know how to thank you." The gratitude curving Bailey's lips into a smile was sweeter than the cheers of every faceless crowd at every football game he'd ever won.

The simplicity of her beauty staggered him.

"There's nothing to thank me for. You and your grandmother need to walk away from losing this place with the chance to start over. I'm happy to help."

Happy.

Instead of advising a megacorporation, he was helping a struggling small business, and insuring that two wonderful women had the hope they deserved.

"I think I'll clean up the last of the dishes and head on upstairs." Mrs. Greenwood took his plate and glass. "I started reading a new mystery last night and can't wait to find out whodunit. Thank you again, Derrick. Next time you stop by, be sure to bring those beautiful little girls of yours."

"Yes, ma'am," he said as she walked away.

"I think you just won yourself a lifetime supply of pie." Bailey fiddled with the V neck of her light blue T-shirt.

Did she have any idea how much he wanted his fingers stroking there instead?

"Well, I definitely won't turn down anything your grandmother gets into her head to bake for me." He walked around the table to sit beside Bailey, and took her hand. "But I'm a selfish man. You know I want more, right?"

Her fingers curled trustingly around his.

"You're angling for another cinnamon roll for breakfast," she teased.

"Breakfast?" The sparkle in her eyes healed him exactly where he needed it most. In the part of his soul that had never been enough—not for his old man, or football, or Amanda or, until recently, his girls.

"I've cancelled my weekend shifts at the Stop Right and at Margo's," she said. "I thought I'd take some time off, since there's no real chance to save this place now. Maybe work on figuring out what's next for me. Would you… Would you like to maybe spend some time together, since the girls will be gone?" She raised both hands in resignation. "I'll understand if—"

"Just try to get rid of me." Standing, he drew her to her feet, then into the kiss he'd been starving for since waking with her in his arms that morning.

BAILEY ARCHED off her bed and into Derrick's embrace, shedding more of her doubts with each caress she returned, each gasp of pleasure that echoed his gruff murmurs.

Wherever Derrick touched, she felt alive. Wherever he looked, she felt radiant. Beautiful. Amazing. Bolder by the second, as she tried to show him, and herself, what she needed. What she'd always needed.

To be free. To finally stop hiding and let herself dream.

And right now, her dream was Derrick.

Her hair curled down her shoulders as she pushed him to his back and straddled his hips. Her fingers gripped the corded muscles in his upper arms as his hands cupped her breasts, giving her more pleasure in one simple touch than any man ever had.

He was a hero.

Everything any woman could want.

And he was completely focused on her. Pulling her head down and kissing her as if he'd starve without another taste.

Then, their gazes locked, and he was there. Deep inside her. Filling her, overwhelming her with the beauty of it, a split second before they both went wild and there was nothing left but a sweet, rough race to give more. Take more. Share everything their bodies knew how to say better than words ever could.

When her climax came, when she couldn't hold herself above him a moment longer, his arms caught her, turned her, trapped her beneath him as he continued to drive her to distraction.

There was no soft landing. No gentle return to reality. Not with Derrick. The determined glint in his eye said he wasn't anywhere near finished.

"Stay with me." He interlaced their fingers and drew her hands over her head. "Don't slip away. Not yet."

His pace quickened. She had no choice but to follow. Her body shot from the misty plateau of completion back to the fiery edges of razor-sharp passion so fast, she cried out. Strained to be free, so she could hold him. Soothe him. Stop what was happening inside her before it was too late, and there was no going back.

He let her go, but only to slide his hands beneath her and pull her more tightly against him.

"Derrick!" In the moonlit shadows of her bedroom, his gorgeous face hardened with desire. Need. The same desperation she was afraid to let rule her.

"Stay with me, Bailey." His rough command was also a plea. One she didn't know how to refuse.

Shoving the fear aside, she lifted her head to capture his lips. She sent her tongue deep, as she wrapped herself more tightly around him and let herself believe that it would be okay in the morning.

That letting herself fall even more deeply in love with this man wasn't going to destroy her, if she couldn't keep the doubt from taking over again.

SUNDAY AFTERNOON had never come faster.

For Derrick, the last thirty-six hours had been pure magic.

He'd ignored repeated calls from Spencer, except once, when he'd explained that he was taking time off unless there was an emergency. Bailey had insisted they play tourist and indulge in the kind of mindless fun neither of them had allowed themselves in years. They'd visited Golden Gate Park. Hooked up with a charter boat that sailed under the bridge. Took a cable-car ride. After afternoon tea at Chinatown's Imperial Tea court, they'd walked for hours, taking in the sights and sounds of the city he couldn't wait to share with his girls.

They'd even made time to listen to her grandmother's recounting of her phone conversation with Mike Grantham. The man's take on the situation sounded dead-on. Beverly would be in good shape, when she countered Premier Spa's offer next week. Hastings Chase Whitney would either have to negotiate, or lose the inn's prime spot overlooking the bay to the next buyer Grantham was sure to line up.

Derrick and Bailey had had two wonderful days and two mind-blowing nights together, but now their stolen weekend was almost over. Sitting together on the Gables porch swing, a breeze from the ocean ruffling the leaves of the trees shading the Victorian's front yard, they were rocking silently, holding hands, neither wanting to let go a second before they had to.

"Is Amanda flying back to Atlanta tonight?" Bailey's fingers clenched for a second.

"I'm not sure." He hated the tension shimmering between them again. The unanswered questions that a weekend couldn't resolve. "She's got a suite in town. She didn't tell me much else, except that she'd have the girls back after dinner tonight."

"What if she decides to stay longer?" Bailey's hand slipped away entirely.

"I don't know why she'd stay. Leslie and Savannah have school, and I'm sure Amanda's got a buttload of social commitments luring her back to Atlanta."

"Maybe her priorities have changed."

"What else would she…" The rest of his sentence caught in his throat. Bailey's raised eyebrow assured him he wasn't misunderstanding. "After the last two days, you can't seriously be worried about me wanting anything to do with her, beyond what's best for the girls."

Bailey's gaze shifted to the lush green lawn of the home that wouldn't be hers for much longer.

"Amanda's not going away, Derrick. Not until she gets whatever she's really after. And with everything I have going on in the next few weeks…"

"You don't need my ex making things even more difficult," he finished for her.

"But a big part of me does need you," she said in an almost-whisper, as if speaking too loudly would break some spell they'd fallen under.

He pulled her into his arms, his cheek resting against the soft hair he'd refused to let her pin up all weekend. "I'll do everything I can to make things easier for you. To keep making things easier for my girls. Even if Amanda tries to cause trouble for us, we simply won't let her. *I* won't let her."

"And if she won't take no for an answer? If she's wishing she never let you and the girls go in the first place?"

"That would require Amanda admitting she was wrong, and she's not capable of that kind of reflection. She'll never be able to see past the next thing she needs to make her feel special."

"Then why isn't she off living the high life with her *next thing* now? The kind of life you keep saying she left you for."

Derrick's only answer was to keep rocking the swing.

Amanda's shock at seeing him and Bailey together Friday morning, her renewed interest in Leslie and Savannah, was nothing more than his ex's latest tactic in her mission to make him feel worthless. She'd never be through punishing him for not living up to her expectations, and she didn't mind using the girls as ammunition.

But thinking back now, she'd seemed more hurt than judgmental on Friday. More lost herself, than pointing her finger at how much he was struggling. Almost as if…

Good Lord.

"Rodney's dumped her." Derrick stopped swinging. "The man always has had more sense than I ever did when it came to women. Although I never understood why he blew off our friendship to be with someone he'd seen chew me up, then spit me out when she decided I was damaged goods."

"Amanda's a beautiful woman. I imagine that's all most men need to see."

"The shortsighted bastards, at least." He turned

Bailey until she faced him. "The lucky ones get a second chance to see beyond the beauty, to what's really important."

She stiffened beneath his kiss.

"Damn it. That came out wrong. You—"

"I want what's best for you, Derrick." Bailey drew away. There was no pulling her back this time. "Whatever it takes for you and your girls to be happy. But I'm not sure you know what that is yet, and with Amanda back in town…"

"Amanda being here isn't best for anyone."

"What about your daughters? What if they decide they want their mother back, and the only way you can make that happen is to move back to Atlanta with them?" Bailey stood. "You need to figure this out, Derrick. The same way I need to figure out what I'm going to do next, without…"

She bit her lip.

"Without what?" He propped his forearms on his thighs and clasped his hands together to keep from reaching for her. Pulling her back.

Without him, her tearful frown said.

"I've hid for years," she said. "Behind my obsession to keep the Gables, because it's what I thought Grams needed. Turns out, losing the inn's going to be a new beginning for her. She's going to be fine. *I'm* the one who's lost. I have no idea what *I* need. *Who* I am." She pulled a hair band out of her pocket and twisted her curls into a ponytail, transforming herself back into the no-nonsense woman he'd first met. The one who moved so quickly from one obligation to the next there was little time for anyone or anything else. "And I have to figure that out, without expecting you to be there for me while you've got your own stuff to work through. That wouldn't be fair to either of us."

"Fair?" He pushed to his feet. The swing banged against the house. "I've just spent the most peaceful, unforgettable two days I've ever known. I've fallen in love with you, and I've let myself believe that you were feeling the same thing. But you think it would be *fairer* for everyone, if we just went our separate ways until we've figured out our *separate* problems?"

"Derrick—"

"Maybe we could hook up again later, is that it? Another weekend special, to tide you over for a while longer?"

Hell, maybe that's what Amanda was sniffing around for. Another taste of the good old days, before she headed back home to deal with Rodney.

"Stop it!" Bailey raised her chin. "I'm not some football groupie looking for a quick lay from an All-American to round out my résumé. I think I'm falling in love with you, too, Derrick. *That's* why I spent the weekend with you."

"Then, why—"

"Because I'm scared." She backed away and glanced down at her blue jeans and T-shirt. "And I don't want to be scared anymore. I just want to *be* for a while. If I don't even know who I am, how can I trust who I am with you? Who I am *to* you. Look at how badly I'm messing this up. We could both use some space—"

"What I could use," Derrick said as he fished his keys from his pocket and headed down the inn's whitewashed front steps, walking away instead of crowding her one more time, "is a woman who wants something besides a golden boy in her bed. Someone who trusts me to help with her problems and to be there for her during the bad times, as well as the good ones."

CHAPTER SIXTEEN

"I FOUND THE INVENTORY you thought was missing,"
Bailey announced as soon as she entered the Stop
Right's office.

Her shift didn't start for hours, but she'd known
Drayton would be there, same as he was every Monday
morning, to check the previous week's receipts. That's
why she'd come in after closing last night and replaced
every last bottle that Leslie's friend had taken.

Time to settle accounts.

"What are you talking about?" He scowled over
the rim of his reading glasses.

"Someone shoved the cases into the corner behind
the door. I missed them, too, when I looked last week."

"There was nothing behind the door. *Someone*
took off with my merchandise."

"Not according to the inventory I did last night.
Everything matches up with what you received from
the distributor, and what we've sold, right down to
the last bottle." She'd made sure of it. "I guess we
both made a mistake."

"You're making a mistake, if you think I'm going to let you cover for that Cavenaugh girl like this."

"Turn Leslie loose, Mr. Drayton. She didn't take anything this time, and she's worked long enough to pay for lifting the condoms. Either start paying her a salary, which I don't even think is legal at her age, or send her home."

"Don't order me around." Drayton shoved to his feet. "This is my store, and I'm about done listening to you tell me what to do."

"No problem. Consider this my two weeks' notice."

"What?"

"I'm out of here, just as soon as you find a replacement."

The grind of shift work no longer held any appeal, now that the Gables was going. She hated this place. She'd always hated it, and she deserved better. She always had.

"Refuse to do right by the Cavenaugh girl," she warned, "and I'm gone, as of now."

"You can't do that! Where am I going to find someone to cover your hours that quickly?"

"Not to mention lining up an accountant to do your books."

"What's that kid to you?" he sneered. "Or is it her daddy you're cozying up to, trying to score some points?"

"Leslie's a good girl." Bailey refused to be baited,

or to let her mind wander in Derrick's direction. She'd done enough of that, while she tossed and turned her sheets into a twisted heap all night. "She's made some bad decisions, but she's learned from her mistakes, and she's done good work here. Send her home, or I walk sooner rather than later."

"You planning on showing up for your shift this afternoon?" Drayton's demand sounded more like a request this time.

"I guess that depends on what you'll be telling Leslie, when she gets here after school."

Bailey held her breath.

Regardless of whatever deal Grams's real estate attorney negotiated for the Gables, another few weeks of Stop Right pay wouldn't hurt their bottom line. It would take Bailey at least that long to pick a new direction, and to figure out if Derrick would be anywhere on her radar once she did—which wasn't at all a given, considering how she'd freaked out on him last night.

"Tell the girl she's done." Drayton shoved past Bailey to get to the door. "I'm going to check the storeroom. Everything had better be where it belongs."

Oh, the booze would be right where it was supposed to be. And now Leslie would be where she belonged in the afternoons—working things out with her family.

That would leave Bailey with the space and the time she'd said she needed.

Too bad she still had no idea where *she* belonged.

"You mean I don't have to come back to this crappy place anymore?" Leslie slapped a hand over her mouth. "Sorry, I know you have to work here, but how can you stand it?"

"That's okay." Bailey grabbed a case of soda like the one she'd handed to Leslie, then led the way out of the storeroom. "I'll be doing my own victory dance in a couple of weeks, when I clock out for the last time."

"You found a better job?"

"I don't know yet," Bailey said with a no-big-deal shrug. "I just know that I'm done here."

Leslie helped her load cans onto the store's refrigerated shelves.

"Done with the Stop Right, or done with Langston?" Her stomach did that tingly, why-did-I-eat-the-lunchroom-meat-loaf thing at the thought that Bailey might actually leave town.

"What do you mean?" Bailey ducked her head back into the cooler to rearrange some things, but not before Leslie caught the weird look on her face.

"I heard my dad and mom arguing last night." Leslie finished unloading her case of soda and let the door she'd been holding open with her hip slam shut. "Mom wanted to know how long Dad was going to keep chasing after someone like you. And he said probably not long, since you were selling the inn."

"Someone like me, huh?" Bailey's cooler door swung shut, too.

"*Is* my dad chasing you?" Leslie followed her back to the storeroom. "Are you selling your house?"

Still no answer.

Leslie grabbed Bailey's arm and spun her around. "You can't leave Langston!"

"This coming from a kid who's done everything short of chartering a plane out of town." Bailey lightly punched her shoulder. "Does that mean you're warming up to the idea of hanging around?"

"I want to stop being such a brat." It wasn't like she *loved* Langston or San Francisco or anything, but she did love her dad. "If that means staying here, then I guess I can do that." She punched Bailey back. "Are you really thinking about leaving?"

A big part of what had made Leslie's day okay during her sentence at the Stop Right had been knowing she'd see Bailey. The woman had stood up for her to everybody. Even Drayton. After today, they wouldn't be working together anymore. And that kind of sucked, no matter how much Leslie wanted out of this place.

"I've been thinking about a lot of things, actually." Bailey brushed the bangs out of Leslie's eyes.

"Things like my dad?"

"Your dad's got a lot to deal with right now, and—"

"It's my mom, isn't it? She's always messing everything up. I wish she'd just die sometimes."

"Don't do that." Bailey sounded angry for the first time since Leslie had met her. "Don't say something you don't mean, just because you've had a rough time. Be pissed. Be a kid, and do all the things that kids do when they're pissed at their parents. But don't wish your mom away. One day, I hope you two can work things out."

"What, and until we do, you can't have anything to do with my family anymore? Is that why you talked your boss into letting me go?"

Disgusted, Leslie headed for the door.

"No." Bailey followed this time, all the way to the office, where Leslie pulled a stick of gum from her backpack. "It's time for you to get back to your life, instead of slaving away here for nothing. You can't work things out with your family when you're spending every afternoon here with me."

"Work things out? My mom ditched us. And now all of a sudden, she wants Savannah and me back? It makes me want to pull out all that hair she has bleached every month."

"She's still your mother," Bailey reasoned.

"Yeah, and I'm still pissed." Leslie had refused to be anything else all weekend.

She'd caused her dad and Bailey so much grief, and now *Amanda* was joining in on the party.

"Is your mom heading home today?" Bailey asked.

"No."

"Well, then, be pissed all you want. But you still have to deal with her."

"Yeah, and you can run from my dad all you want, but you're still going to have to deal with me." Leslie handed her a piece of gum.

The kind she'd noticed Bailey liked the best.

"Well, then." Bailey unwrapped it, then smiled as she dropped into the office chair and popped the gum into her mouth. "Sounds like we both have stuff to work on."

Leslie sat in the guest chair.

"You can't move away," she said. "You grew up here. How can you leave everyone and everything you know?"

"I was supposed to leave a long time ago, sweetie." Bailey sounded like a kid herself. "And maybe there's nowhere to go anymore. But I promised myself that if I ever got the chance, I'd try, even if it was too late."

"Too late for what?"

"Whatever."

"So you're gone, just like that?" Like Leslie cared. Like she cared about any of this.

Bailey sat forward, her expression as intense as it had been the day she'd caught Leslie shoplifting and had sat there nagging at her until her dad arrived.

"Not every adult bails on the people they're supposed to care about," Bailey said, "just because they think life'll be more fun somewhere else. I'm not going anywhere. Not until I'm sure my grandmother's settled and happy."

Swallowing suddenly hurt. Leslie rooted around with her tongue to make sure she still had her gum.

"My mom doesn't care about anyone but herself," she finally said. "She didn't even care when we moved out here."

"Maybe she's changed her mind." Bailey blew a bubble and winked. "But if she hasn't, you let me know, and I'll give you a hand with that hair pulling."

Leslie grinned and blew her own bubble.

"So is your grandmother the only reason you're sticking around for a while?" she asked. "What about my dad?"

"Leslie, your dad and I—"

"You're perfect for each other—"

"Leslie…"

"I've seen the way you look at him."

"It's not that simple. I—"

"I've seen the way he looks at you."

"Leslie." Bailey sat back. "I'm not like…"

"Not like what?"

"I… I'm not like your mom or any of the other women your dad's used to being around."

"Thank God!" a voice said from over Leslie's

shoulder. Selena walked in and bent down to give Leslie a hug. "Your dad asked me to pick you up, sweetie. He said he'd meet you at home. Grab your stuff. Drew and Axel are outside destroying what's left of my Honda."

"If Dad already left work early," Leslie asked, "why didn't he come get me himself?"

"He didn't say." Selena glanced toward Bailey. "Any ideas?"

Bailey started to answer, then stopped.

"She's worried about how she looks," Leslie told Selena. "And she thinks Dad—"

"I'm not *worried*," Bailey argued. "Not about your father. I know he likes me the way I am, however I dress, but I..." Bailey stopped fiddling with her shirt. "I don't. I haven't for a long time, and until I do..."

"Well, that's certainly fixable." Selena nudged Leslie's shoulder. "What do you say about doing our very own version of *What Not to Wear* this weekend?"

"Can we talk?" asked the striking blonde on Derrick's doorstep.

She'd always be beautiful. She'd always be the center of attention in whatever room she walked into. But Derrick had never been more certain that he was over his ex-wife.

His idea of beautiful now included brains and a

gentle spirit. Someone whose inner glow made everything on the outside sparkle a little more. Bailey's kind of glow. The kind that the put-together woman standing before him couldn't buy, no matter how many beauty salons she haunted for the latest treatments and potions.

"Come on in." He stepped back, opening the door wider.

"Are the girls home?" Amanda asked.

"Savannah headed next door to play when she got off the bus, and Leslie should be home soon from the convenience store." He'd asked Selena to pick her up. Bailey said she needed space, and he didn't trust himself not to fly off the handle again if he saw her, the way he had yesterday. "If you wanted to see the girls, you should have called to let me know you were coming."

"Actually, I wanted to see you." Amanda set her purse on the coffee table. "I had a lot of thinking to do first, and, well… After my last trip, and everything we said to each other Friday and last night, I wasn't sure if you'd agree to talking, so I—"

"You figured you'd drop by when the kids were here and reduce the chances that I'd throw you out?"

Amanda swallowed. She sat on the edge of the couch.

"I'm trying to do this peacefully, Derrick, for our children's sake. I know I've been out of the loop for a while, and I feel terrible about that. I came back this weekend to try and reconnect with them, but Leslie won't talk to me. And Savannah always copies everything her sister does, and—"

"So you being back here doesn't have anything to do with Rodney not coming home last week between his road games. Or the fact that you were supposed to be in Dallas with him this weekend, but a different blonde was on his arm in the post-game party photos?"

Derrick slammed the front door.

Amanda's smile was well-rehearsed perfection. "Rodney socializes with all kinds of women at these events. He laughs with me about it every night when he calls. And I couldn't possibly go with him on every out-of-town trip. I'd be bored out of my mind."

"Yes, parties and paparazzi and a new excuse to buy clothes three-fourths of the people in the country can't afford have always bored you in the past." A few calls to his NFL contacts had yielded a ton of rumors, and enough facts to piece together the rest. "Did Rodney start sleeping around on you before or after he realized you were only with him for his money and the big-time lifestyle you can't have without it?"

Moisture pooled in the corners of Amanda's eyes.

"Derrick—"

"Don't. Don't bother with the tears. You came to the wrong place looking for sympathy."

"We're only taking a break." Amanda's ice-princess calm returned. "We agreed to take some time to decide what we want. And all I could think about while I was alone last week was the girls. You were right to be angry with me for dropping in unannounced for the Western–Langston game, and for not coming before then. I can see how unhappy the children are, and I want to help change that. I think they're what I've been missing over the last year. Maybe that's why things aren't working out in Atlanta without them."

"So, now making more time for the kids is going to fix your relationship with the man who convinced you it would be better if I took them instead?" Derrick wasn't sure which had shocked him more, the girls' *Uncle Rodney* breaking up what was left of their parents' marriage, or the man not wanting to have anything to do with the kids once he had.

"I'm thinking about what's best for Leslie and Savannah right now, not me."

"Don't you always." It was clear where this friendly conversation was headed. "If you think for one minute that I'm going to let you—"

"You said yourself that things aren't going well. Leslie's in trouble—"

"We've dealt with that. Leslie and I are doing better." Thanks to a woman who still couldn't trust herself, or the love she'd shown him how to feel again.

"But you're still working until all hours of the night, seven days a week."

"I'll be here every afternoon after school from now on, and I'm cutting back my weekend hours. The girls need me home, so that's where I'll be."

"And how long do you expect to keep pulling that off, and still have your job at Hastings Chase Whitney?"

"Not very long, considering that I was just pulled from the case I've been managing since I moved here. My promotion's pretty much trashed. I figure it'll take them another six months or so to find a reason for firing me that HR can live with." Less than that, if Premier Spa lost the Gables Inn deal and someone looked close enough to wonder if Derrick was partially responsible. "I'm due for a nice severance bonus, but I'm looking for a job outside of corporate law, starting tomorrow."

"Right, the Mighty DC is giving up his big-time prospects to play in the bar leagues."

"I'm as serious as I can be." He had no idea what his next career move was. But it was going to be one that allowed him to be a successful father first, before anything else. "The girls and I are going to be fine here, so no worries. You can head back to Atlanta and patch up your marriage any way you like. We don't need your help."

Amanda actually snorted.

"Let me get this straight. You've been a no-show

as a parent since Leslie was born. You've had our children all to yourself for a year, and you've failed miserably. But now that you're finally serious about making someone besides yourself a priority, you're instantly a contender for Father of the Year…. Have I missed anything?"

By the time she'd finished, Amanda's tone had sharpened to just the right pitch to obliterate any shred of guilt Derrick still harbored for taking their marriage for granted.

"My priorities are right where they need to be," he said, remembering what his new single-parent friends had said. "They have been ever since I decided to move the girls to Langston. I've made mistakes, and I'm sure I'll make more. But I'm learning, and I plan to make this work."

"And where, exactly, do I fit in these plans?"

"*You* divorced *me*, Amanda."

"You were long gone, years before that."

"You'd been sleeping with Rodney for months. You got remarried a week after our divorce was finalized, then you couldn't get rid of the girls fast enough."

"It was my turn to be selfish for a while! I finally took some time for what I needed." It was the same old argument, from the same warped viewpoint. "You should know a little something about that, DC!"

"Everyone in your world is being selfish according to you." He actually found himself feeling sorry for her. "No matter what anyone does, it's never going to be enough. There couldn't possibly be enough attention, enough time or enough money to satisfy you."

"Like you ever tried." Shadows swam behind the real tears filling Amanda's eyes. "Like you ever really cared about what I needed, as long as I kept pretending to be happy, so you could get on with the career that was going to make up for losing your chance to play pro ball."

"Believe it or not, I did care, even though I never did enough to show it."

He'd focused too much on providing the material things he'd thought she and the girls needed. But he'd always cared. It had taken falling in love with Bailey, and the way she saw the world, for him to realize that his heart and his time were the most precious things he could give the people in his life.

"Well, I *don't* believe you." Amanda stood and picked up her purse. "And I'm not leaving my children here any longer to be emotionally abandoned the way I was."

"You're not…" It was Derrick's turn to snort. "You made your choice when you walked away from your family. Just because you're miserable and alone and need to boost your ego by playing Mommy again, doesn't mean everything goes back to the way it was before."

"According to our divorce agreement, I have joint custody. We were both supposed to remain living in the Atlanta area, while we raised our children together."

"There was no *together* anymore, so I took the heat for them not being able to see you, and removed them from the situation. Leslie's figured out the truth, but at least Savannah's not completely aware that her mother didn't care whether she stayed or not."

"I just—"

"Needed some time, right. How much time do you think Rodney's going to need? What happens if he decides he wants you back, and the girls are in the way again?"

"I won't let that happen."

"Like hell you won't! I'm not letting you take the girls back to Atlanta, just so you can shove them aside again when the mood strikes. Go patch things up with your husband, or find yourself a new meal ticket. Leslie and Savannah can visit you as often as it fits into their school schedule. Or you can move closer to us. But their home is here with me now. Period."

"I think a judge will see things differently." Amanda pulled a legal-size envelope from her purse. "This is a letter from my attorney, requesting that you return the girls to Atlanta, as stipulated in our custody agreement. And that we resume a schedule that splits their time evenly between us. Otherwise, I'll petition the court for sole custody."

Derrick took the envelope and crumpled it in his fist.

"I won't let you do this. I won't let you rip my family apart again."

"Stop being so dramatic, Derrick. This is what you wanted all along—me taking care of the girls, so you could get on with your life."

"That's not true," he whispered.

But the flicker of shame that shimmered through him was a reminder of all the times over the last year that he'd wished for just that, if only to save his daughters from him screwing things up even more.

"Of course it's true. Let me take them home. Get back to whatever superimportant deal you've got brewing. Bop your little convenience-store clerk until your eyes cross. I'm offering you the chance of a lifetime to ditch a responsibility you never wanted. *I'll* take the heat this time. Pretend it's all my idea. All you have to do is pack up the girls' things, and we'll call it even."

"No!" Leslie shouted from the front door neither Derrick nor Amanda had heard open. She was staring at Derrick with the same shocked expression as when he'd announced they were moving to the West Coast. "You can't do this. I won't go back to Atlanta. I won't!"

Turning, shoving Selena aside, Leslie sprinted down the sidewalk, her sobs ringing through the now-silent house.

CHAPTER SEVENTEEN

DERRICK DROPPED the duffel bag beside the Langston baseball field's bleachers and fitted the extra ball cap he'd been carrying on his daughter's head.

"It's a good thing you're back to dressing like a kid again," he said. "Means you don't have to go home and change first. Come on, let's see what you've got."

Leslie didn't move, didn't look up.

He'd headed for the ball field on a hunch. Had mentally patted himself on the back when Leslie had in fact been there, consoling himself that maybe he wasn't a total loser as a father, after all.

That moment was definitely over.

So was the raging need he'd had on the way over to blame this latest setback on Amanda.

The truth was, he'd destroyed his daughter's trust a long time ago, and it would take a whole lot more than a change of heart on his part to earn it back.

"All I have is baseballs, but we should be able to work something out." He fished bats and gloves from the bag and headed for the deserted field. "Bailey said you've been interested in playing softball since we moved here."

Leslie finally looked up.

"Was that before or after you ran her off, just like you did Mom?"

Derrick took his turn staring at the packed ground beneath home plate.

"You have every right to be mad at Mom and me." He walked back and sat on the bench beside his daughter. "But don't be angry at Bailey."

"Why would I be angry at Bailey! It's not like I'm going to be here much longer, anyway."

Derrick grabbed the bill of Leslie's cap and tugged until she looked at him.

"You and your sister aren't going anywhere. Not without me."

"Because I've made the last year such a blast for you, right?" There was more insecurity than sass in her comeback.

Derrick wrapped his arm around her shoulder before he could worry that he was making a mistake. When she didn't resist, but instead laid her head against his chest, this child who'd run from him every way she could, he hugged her closer.

"Because I can't imagine not having you girls with me. I've already missed so much with you and your sister. I won't miss any more. I can't."

He heard a distinct sniffle and patted her shoulder, determined to hold on until she was ready to let go. It took several minutes, and three or four deep breaths, before Leslie inched away. And still it was too soon.

"Mom sounded really angry."

"I guess she has a right to be."

"Not after what she did to all of us."

"I messed things up plenty before the divorce, Leslie. It took me way too long to realize what was really important in my life. But now that I do, I won't make those mistakes again. I promise."

Leslie's nod of agreement was full of such simple understanding and forgiveness, he wanted to lock the moment away forever.

"But what about Bailey?" she asked. "She's worked it out so I don't have to go back to the Stop Right, but now she's quitting. And she's talking about maybe leaving San Francisco, and…"

Bailey had set Leslie free.

And now she might be leaving herself, after laying in his arms just yesterday morning.

"She's been a good friend," was all Derrick could manage.

A friend who'd helped give Leslie another chance to be the great kid she was meant to be, and made sure Derrick got *his* second chance with both of his girls.

A friend who deserved the future she'd always wanted, no matter how hard it would be to let her go.

"Not you, too!" Leslie stomped down the bleachers and rounded on him. "You mean to tell me, that you spent the entire weekend being *friends,* while Savannah and I were with Mom! Do friends snuggle the way you two were Friday morning? I'm not a baby, Dad. I know what Mom thought you were doing. I know why she's so steamed right now. It's not about getting me and Savannah back, it's about you and your *friend,* Bailey."

"No." Derrick pulled his own hat from the back pocket of his jeans and stalled putting it on, until he was sure he could focus on what his daughter needed to hear, instead of his ex-wife's bitchiness. "It's about how much your mother cares about you and your sister, and how much she misses you."

"Like she even thought about us before last week."

"She thought about you," Derrick said as he stood. "She just—"

"Had better things to do than be with us? What happens when she changes her mind again, and then—"

"Then we'll deal with it." He took Leslie's hand and squeezed. "Together. You're not getting rid of me. Wherever you go, I go. Deal?"

Leslie started to say something, but stopped and squeezed his hand back. Looking at the ground, she kicked the duffel bag.

"So what's all this?"

"You said you wanted to learn how to play ball." He steered her toward the equipment he'd left at home plate.

"Didn't you bring work home to do?" She picked up a glove.

"Nope, no more work tonight." And somehow he'd find a way to ensure there'd be many more nights where his beautiful girls were his only focus. "Your mom's taking Savannah out for a while, and you're all mine until dinnertime. So how 'bout it?"

"Really?" Leslie's face lit up as she slipped the glove on.

"Really."

Stepping onto a sports field for the first time since his injury, he began to explain the basics of the game. And it felt good. It was humbling, actually, to see his love for baseball shining back at him from his child's eyes. He actually laughed out loud at the freedom of it.

He and his girls were going to be fine. He was as sure of that now as he'd been convinced he was failing as a father just a few weeks ago. He'd even find a way to work with Amanda, so their daughters would no longer be the collateral damage from their parents' divorce. And he was going to make the time to learn from other parents, from his own kids, until he had this *dad* thing licked.

And once he did, he'd have everything.

Everything, but a remarkable woman with a bright,

unrealized future ahead of her, who didn't know what she wanted to do with a rookie single-father who hadn't quite recovered from his social coma.

"WE HAVE A LIGHT CROWD this weekend," Bailey said over muffins Saturday morning, "but are you sure you won't need me?"

"I've got it under control." Grams smiled as she spoke. She hadn't stopped smiling, actually, since her meeting with Mike Grantham.

"I know you do."

Being in control suited her grandmother. Knowing that Premier Spa was going to have to pony up with a much better offer—seeing Grantham's list of a half a dozen other investors that were already interested in the Gables—had taken a lot of the sting out of selling.

"You go on and enjoy your day with Selena and Leslie. It sounds like fun."

"Yeah, fun." What wasn't fun about being a fashion misfit so clueless she was turning her *look,* as Selena called it, over to a twelve-year-old and a new friend she'd only met a month ago?

"I know all this change is hard for you, honey." Grams's excitement took a turn toward serious. "Nothing's worked out the way you expected it to."

Bailey had thought a lot over the last week about what would have happened if she'd rushed off to college, and then to the career she'd dreamed of. Of all the time she'd have missed with this loving woman who'd been the only mother she'd ever known. Bailey had let herself feel trapped for so long, when what she'd been *stuck* in was experiencing the kind of support and love a lot of people never knew.

She took her grandmother's hand. "But I think I'm starting to understand that surprises don't always have to be such scary things."

"You've never stopped surprising me, from the moment your parents brought you home from the hospital." Her grandmother's eyes sparkled with pride. "You've given up so much for me, Bailey. I can't wait to give you back your chance to have everything you always wanted."

"You don't owe me anything." Tit-for-tat reciprocity was the last thing Bailey wanted.

"Just seven years' salary. Years you should have been off building your career. That's why I asked Mr. Grantham to structure whatever deal he makes, so that half of what's left after the IRS takes its cut goes to you."

"Grams!" The coffee Bailey was sipping tried to resurface through her nose. She forced it down. "That's *your* money. Your retirement."

"No, it's Greenwood family money. And half of everything I have is yours, Bailey. More than half. I'd never have recovered from losing Adam, if it weren't for you."

"But—"

"That's the way things are going to be, young lady." Grams hadn't "young-ladied" her since Bailey was in high school. "You're going to college, if that's what you want. Whatever college you want. I'll accept nothing less. You gave me the time and support I needed to get back on my feet. Now it's my turn to help."

"But the business you said you wanted to start…" Bailey's nose was burning again, with little-girl sniffles this time, not coffee. "I'm not taking the chance to do that away from you."

"No. You never take anything for yourself." Her grandmother didn't sound proud anymore. She sounded worried. "And it's time you learned how. This is the way it's going to be, honey. Your father would have wanted you to have your dreams, too. I've made up my mind."

The buzzer at the front desk sounded.

"Go spend the day with your friends," Grams said, as if Bailey were a kid again, and she had nothing more to worry about than a weekend playdate. "Give doing exactly what you want a chance. We can talk about the rest later."

Exactly what you want…

As if Bailey had a clue what that was.

But as she headed for the foyer, she knew the one thing she wanted for certain was for someone else to be waiting for her at the front desk. Someone besides a beautiful local artist and an adorably smart-mouthed twelve-year-old.

Someone who knew what it was like to lose himself in the surprising twists and turns life too often took. Someone who'd been battling through the mess, and often failing, for nearly as long as Bailey had.

CHAPTER EIGHTEEN

"Wow, LOOK HOW LONG your legs look," Leslie said in awe.

"It's the shoes," Selena agreed.

The woman's feet were the same size as Bailey's, and she'd brought what seemed like an entire shoe store over for Bailey to try on.

"With your killer calves," Selena continued, "you should wear heels as often as you can."

"This skirt doesn't hurt." Bailey could wear most of Selena's clothes. Except the pants, which swallowed up Bailey's petite frame. "I've never worn anything this short."

"That's not short." Leslie wrinkled her nose at the way the hem of the black skirt ended just above Bailey's knees. "Ginger has some that you can see her panties when she bends over."

"A ringing endorsement." Bailey twirled the girl around. Leslie was wearing a hip pair of skinny jeans and a vintage-looking T-shirt with a 70s rock-star logo on it. Plus a *kicky* pair of slides, as Leslie put it. "This is definitely less likely to give your dad a coronary."

"You should try some jeans like that," Selena suggested.

"I don't have the body for it." And wasn't it an ego boost that a twelve-year-old was sporting more curves than Bailey.

"They're stretch," Leslie explained, as if that said it all.

"They pull up what you have and give it shape in all the right places," Selena translated. "You couldn't possibly have less going on back there than Leslie, and she looks great in them."

"Hey!" Leslie's double-take was priceless.

"I think we've both been insulted, kiddo," Bailey commiserated.

"You should borrow them. I have to change anyway." Leslie disappeared into Bailey's bathroom, where they'd first played with Bailey's hair, and then her makeup. For the last hour, it had become a changing room, as Bailey slowly nudged her fashion sense into the new millennium.

Selena began gathering up the tops and skirts and shoes and dresses she'd brought over after dropping her son and their dog off at a friend's for the morning.

"Change for what?" Bailey looked away from the distraction of her made-over reflection in the vanity mirror, just in time to catch the jeans Leslie tossed out of the bathroom.

The girl emerged wearing the Western High T-shirt Bailey had given her and a pair of simple cotton shorts.

"My dad's picking me up in a few minutes." She was grinning from ear-to-ear as she sat down to change into sneakers. "He's taking Savannah and me to Golden Gate Park for a picnic and to play some softball."

"That's great, honey." Selena glanced Bailey's way.

"It's wonderful," Bailey agreed.

And also disturbing.

Derrick would be there any minute....

And now Leslie was looking at her, too. Expectantly. The little minx had set her up.

Bailey ducked into the bathroom, stalling in front of the mirror as she had so many times since that morning.

Tossing large hot rollers into her hair had helped tame the out-of-control curls that usually left her reaching for something to put it up with. Nutmeg and vanilla colored shadows, expertly applied by Leslie, had made her eyes look larger and a more vibrant green. And subtle shades of pink and rose had her cheeks and lips glowing.

Add into the mix the sleeveless emerald sweater and the startling fit of the jeans Bailey had slipped on, and she looked like...

She looked like the woman Derrick's touch had always made her feel she was.

Almost a week had passed since she'd insisted on needing time. Leslie had mentioned Amanda's return to Atlanta. But was the woman really gone? Was Derrick really free of the stress his ex had been causing his family for years? Free enough to know for certain what he wanted next?

"What do you think?" Selena called from the bedroom.

"It's…" Bailey emerged, looking over her shoulder at her butt. "I never knew jeans could look this way." Not on her. "Where's Leslie?"

Selena nodded toward the window that overlooked the front yard and driveway.

"She heard her dad pull up. I guess she figured she'd spare you from having to answer the door."

Bailey stayed glued to the spot, wanting desperately to rush to the window, but refusing to let herself. Selena headed into the bathroom to clean up the last of their clutter.

"You know," the other woman said, "I'm into you doing all this for yourself. Seeing what you might want before you buy some new things of your own. But it might be fun to show off your look to someone else."

So much fun, Bailey had been hiding in the bathroom just now.

She parted her sunny yellow curtains in time to watch Derrick's Lexus pull out of the drive and head for the city.

Give doing exactly what you want a chance.

Her grandmother's advice hadn't left Bailey alone all day. Neither had memories of Derrick, as Leslie chattered away about her dad. The girl who'd spent the last year insisting she didn't care what her dad thought about anything was now over the moon because he was teaching her how to play ball.

Of course, what Derrick and Leslie had been through was more complicated than that, but their happy ending was as simple as it got. Leslie had found a way to trust in the terrifying process of starting over. And a struggling single father had finally accepted the life he really wanted, and he'd keep fighting until he got it, no matter how many times he messed up along the way.

They'd taken the kind of leap of faith Bailey still couldn't.

After eleven years of seeing herself as a survivor, it was hell to realize she'd been hiding the whole time. Refusing to take any chance that risked losing. To approach any cliff she might be tempted to jump off.

The shock of her father's sudden death had been enough to last Bailey a lifetime. Setting herself up to potentially lose again, in love or in whatever life she might have had away from Grams and the Gables, had been too risky. So she'd focused every waking moment on surviving, instead. Enduring. Until she'd lost even the memory of wanting more.

"Is that really what I want?" she asked the window she'd gazed out of every morning since she was a little girl.

"What?" Selena asked from the bathroom door. When Bailey shook her head instead of answering, her friend stepped closer. "You look great in that. How does it feel?"

"Lonely," was the only word Bailey could find.

She gazed down at her borrowed fashion, and she finally got it.

Why all morning, every glance at her reflection had been so unsettling. The outer changes Selena and Leslie had helped her make were heckling at everything she'd refused to let herself be on the inside.

Brave.

Confident.

Ready to face whatever cliffs loomed ahead.

The kind of Bailey Derrick had tempted her to be from the moment he'd barged back into her life.

"GREAT STROKE." Derrick laughed out loud at Leslie's major-league grunt as she made contact.

The softball sailed over his head.

"I got it." Savannah ran off, wearing an old glove that was so big it kept sliding off her hand.

"You really got your hips into that one." He gave Leslie a high five, then he turned her by the shoulders until she was standing sideways again. "Now this time, bend your knees, and don't let them straighten as your upper body pivots into the swing. Twist at your waist and step toward the ball, pushing off your back foot. But stay down all the way through the swing."

"Cool!" Leslie was beaming, ready to do whatever he asked her to next.

They'd been at it for over an hour. If he left it up to Leslie, they'd probably still be there after dark. Not that he minded. He was falling in love with baseball all over again, through his daughter's eager eyes.

He stepped back to pitch as Savannah ran up.

"Can I try, Daddy?"

"Sure, honey." Having both his girls so excited to be spending time with him—*him*—grabbed at his heart. He cleared his throat, and wiped a drop of what must have been sweat from his eyes. "We'll switch it up soon, and let Leslie pitch a few to you."

Hastings wasn't speaking to him. Derrick's days at the firm were clearly numbered. He hadn't seen Bailey since last Sunday. She may have completely written him off, too, and he had no right to go after her. Not after everything she'd already done for him.

But despite all he'd failed at, he'd never felt more like the champion his father had wanted him to be.

His kids were spending a day at the park with him and loving it. As if they'd rather be there than anywhere else. That made him an all-star, hands down, no matter how badly he failed in anything else in his life.

Turning back to their makeshift home plate, letting the sunshine and the cool, bay breeze wash over him, he winked at Leslie.

"Okay, weight on your back foot and step into the swing as you make contact with the ball."

She nodded and pulled the bat back, high and away from her shoulder, just as he'd shown her.

The kid was going to be good.

Tossing underhanded, he was momentarily distracted by the gorgeous body of the woman walking toward them. Her sexy hair, and the delicately curved body showcased in a chic top and hip-hugging jeans, were as killer a combo as the giving heart and boundless spunk he'd already fallen in love with.

Lord, she was—

Smack!

Derrick had mere seconds to process the line drive missiling toward him. He slid to the grass as the ball whizzed past his left ear.

"Dad!"

"Derrick!"

Bailey reached him first.

"Are you all right?" she asked.

Her hands on his chest, she leaned closer, and he couldn't resist.

Twisting, he turned her, until she lay on the ground

beneath him. The kiss he gave her had to be quick, given their audience, but it was more than he'd thought he might ever have again. And when Bailey returned it, cupping his jaw and smiling, he started to hope all over again.

"What are you doing here?" he asked.

Leslie had said Bailey and Selena were planning to go to some salon in town to get Bailey's hair cut.

Bailey's eyes sparkled, their beauty accented by the kind of makeup that did its job, even though you could barely tell it was there. Something else was new, too. Her face was lit up with a combination of daring and confidence that he'd never seen before.

"I'm following my dreams." She threaded her fingers through his hair. "Know any ex-jocks with a weakness for terrified women who like to jump off cliffs?"

EPILOGUE

"ANOTHER WEDDING!" Margo cried.

Out of her chair, circling the table, she threw her arms around Derrick, then took Bailey's hand to inspect her sparkling engagement ring.

"That's wonderful."

Bailey soaked in her former boss's delight, as well as the sensation of finally being a customer at the bistro, rather than part-time help. She had her own too-good-to-be-true life to believe in now, instead of secretly envying Margo hers.

She smiled as Robert made his way toward the group, from where he'd been serving Cokes to Leslie and Savannah at the counter. He kissed Bailey's cheek, shook Derrick's hand, then gave his shoulder a manly pat.

"Congratulations," Nora and Rosie said in unison. The women were sitting on either side of Selena.

When Derrick had learned that Selena and the rest of the single-parent group was hooking up at Margo's that morning, he'd wanted to stop by on the way to Leslie's Saturday softball game. He'd surprised Bailey with his proposal last night, just as dusk settled on the front porch of the inn. After sharing the news with Grams and the girls, they'd called Selena, then sworn her to secrecy until they could tell the rest of the friends Derrick had grown close to over the last month.

"You've all been so great to me," he said as Robert hugged Margo to his side. "I should have taken Selena's advice and forced myself to ask for help sooner, but—"

"But why ruin a perfectly good track record of listening to me only after you've exhausted all other avenues?" Selena winked over the rim of her espresso.

She'd supported and then gently prodded Derrick to be a better father, ever since he'd moved back to San Francisco. And she hadn't thought twice before she made room for Bailey in their special bond of friendship. Selena was a fighter who grabbed hold of everything she could get from life, and she expected nothing less from the people she cared about. Bailey felt unbelievably lucky to be included in that company.

Derrick was smiling at the group circled around the table. Actually, his smile hadn't dimmed since she'd said yes to his proposal. Neither had her heart rate. He raised an eyebrow as his gaze settled on the pulse galloping away at the base of her throat. He raised her fingers to his lips for a kiss.

Robert chuckled. "I take it this won't be a long engagement."

"It's going to be a Christmas wedding," Leslie answered. She and Savannah were both excited about their dad's announcement. But Leslie had been up at the crack of dawn, scouring the Internet and printing checklists from every wedding planning site she could find. "That's a ton of stuff to do in just three months, but we'll make it."

Bailey's eyes misted.

Having the girls' unquestioning acceptance of her being a part of their father's life, their *family,* was a priceless gift.

"We'd love it if you could cater the reception," Derrick said to Margo and Robert. Then he let his gaze travel around the table. "It'll be a small ceremony, but we were hoping all of you could come."

Smiles and affirmations were instantly offered.

Bailey squeezed his hand, knowing how important the group had become to him. The first night he'd joined them, he'd expected to be seen as an ex-jock. A minor celebrity to be pitied for how badly his life had turned out, and gossiped about once he left. Instead, the group of rock-solid friends had welcomed him, no questions asked. And every time he'd hooked up with them since, the result had been the same.

He belonged. Anytime. And through him, Bailey did, too.

"I hate to do this—" Derrick picked up the to-go cups of coffee he and Bailey had ordered "—but Leslie has a game."

"I'm pitching!" Leslie announced. Long gone was the sarcastic kid who'd first glared at Bailey at the Stop Right.

The girls sprinted for the door. Bailey and Derrick exchanged more hugs and handshakes, promising to be in touch with everyone about wedding details. Once outside, they took their time heading for the parking garage. Bailey looked up to find Derrick watching his daughters walk ahead, a touch of sadness pulling at his smile.

"You okay?" She wrapped her arm around his waist, wishing she could shut out everything but the happiness of the last few minutes.

He hadn't wanted to bring it up to the group yet, but Amanda had phoned not long after he'd proposed, reality and the past intruding on their special moment.

"It's only a long weekend," Bailey reasoned.

"Three days." He said it like it was three months, instead of the Columbus Day weekend Amanda had insisted she get to spend with the girls in Atlanta. "How do I know she'll actually spend time with them? That Rodney won't complain and make them feel like they're not welcome?"

"You don't."

Amanda had patched up whatever was wrong with her marriage, and she'd made good on her threat to try and take the girls back full-time. Her lawyer had advised starting with asking Derrick for a few long weekends. Derrick hadn't had any choice but to agree, if he wanted to avoid a nasty custody battle that would hurt the girls more than anyone else.

"She's their mother," Bailey reasoned. "Savannah's excited about going back to Atlanta for a few days. Even Leslie doesn't seem too upset by the idea. She's already calling her old girlfriends to plan a trip to the mall."

"Yeah," Derrick agreed. "I'm just going to miss them. And what if…"

"What if they decide they want to stay there?" Bailey punched his shoulder. "You seem to be forgetting that your daughters are as in love with you as I am."

"Is that so?" He kissed a sizzling path from her neck to the sensitive spot behind her ear.

"Grams, too. She says she's going to name a pie after you, once the sale is closed and she's settled into the new house."

A modest ranch just two blocks away from the inn, with a bay view, a wraparound porch and an industrial-grade kitchen. All of which would be paid for in full, just from Grams's share of the proceeds from the sale.

"She's been talking me up all around town," Derrick said. "I'm already getting calls from potential clients."

When a lawyer of Derrick's caliber ditched corporate America for private practice, news traveled fast.

Just last week, he'd given notice at Hastings Chase

Whitney. They'd offered him three months paid leave to job search, but it was common knowledge that he was off the market. He was striking out on his own, to fight for everyday clients *and* the family life he wanted with his girls—and with Bailey now, too.

"It might not be so bad." She kissed his cheek, loving the way he closed his eyes to savor the sensation. "We'd have the weekend all to ourselves. We could get a hotel room in the city, maybe at the St. Francis. Maybe hook up with a campus tour, then find a place to hang out and act like a couple of crazy-in-love students for a while."

An Ivy League education held little appeal now. Not when San Francisco University offered a six-year program that suited Bailey just fine. There, she could earn a Bachelor of Science in Accounting, in conjunction with an MBA, all in Langston's, and Derrick Cavenaugh's, backyard.

"Are you trying to distract me?" he whispered in her ear as their steps slowed.

The girls had stopped just ahead to wait for a green light.

"Is it working?" she asked.

He deepened the sweet kiss she offered into more than she'd expected, just like he'd made everything else in her life more special than she'd dreamed it could be.

"I guess it is," she murmured, once his lips lifted.

"We could meet up with Selena for dinner that

weekend," he offered. "Maybe stop by the church to make final arrangements for the wedding."

She'd become Mrs. Bailey Cavenaugh the second weekend in December, with Grams giving her away, and Leslie and Savannah and Selena in her wedding party. Then she and Derrick would head off for a two-week honeymoon in the Caribbean, while the girls spent the holiday with their mother—another of Amanda's requests via her Atlanta lawyer.

"Whatever we do is fine with me," Bailey said. "As long as we're together. If you want to go to Atlanta for Columbus Day in case the girls need you, I'll understand."

She knew he'd been thinking about it. He'd have to fly over with Leslie and Savannah anyway, then Amanda was supposed to chaperone on the flight back. But Derrick could cover both legs of the trip, and he and Bailey could—

"No." He watched the girls as they waited at the curb, all smiles and dressed for an afternoon at the ball park. "Leslie and Savannah need to know that I trust their mother. They deserve whatever relationship they can have with Amanda, and I'd only be in the way if I hung around."

He was still a warrior who'd fight to the death for what was important to him. But somewhere over the last few months, Derrick had learned how to pick his battles, and that made him even more of a champion to Bailey.

"So what's it going to be for lunch?" he asked the girls as they headed across the street to the parking garage. "Hot dogs at the park, or pizza on the way home?"

Home.

Bailey would be moving into Derrick's next week, when the sale to Premier Spa closed. As she said goodbye to the home she'd cherished her entire life, she and Grams were becoming part of a totally new family. A new future full of more love and promise than Bailey ever dared imagine.

"Pizza!" the girls cheered together.

The morning sun was rising higher in the sky, and a cool breeze promised another crisp San Francisco day. So much was changing. The world Bailey had clung to so desperately would soon be gone. But there was no room for anything but excitement in its wake.

Far from being the risk she'd once thought it would be, giving Derrick Cavenaugh her heart had become the safest choice she'd ever made. Because he and his girls had given Bailey back what her father had always wanted for her.

What she'd thought she'd lost forever, when she'd lost him.

Her dreams.

* * * * *

Only two singles are left in the
SINGLES WITH KIDS *club!*
Look for Rosie's story,
THE BEST-KEPT SECRET (SR#1416)
by Melinda Curtis, in May 2007,
wherever Harlequin books are sold.
Turn the page for a sneak peek....

CHAPTER ONE

"I NEED YOU TO DO something for me." A small favor. A phone call. Still, it went against Hudson McCloud's grain to ask anyone for help. It came down to this: swallow his pride and ask his mother for help…or wait. And Hud was done waiting.

"What is it?" Vivian McCloud turned from the skyscraper's view of the turbulent waters of San Francisco Bay and the few sailboats that braved the post Christmas Pacific Ocean tides. His mother had once been full of life, but the events of the past ten years had taken their toll.

And Hud was partially to blame.

He couldn't turn back the clock and prevent the mistakes and losses he'd suffered from happening, but after two years of biding his time there was finally a chance he could restore his family's honor.

Hud crossed the Oriental carpet in his mother's office to the cabinet that held the TV and filled the room with a sound he had come to loathe—a newscast.

"…sad news for the city. San Francisco's mayor

was about to deliver a speech on the steps of city hall when he suffered a brain aneurysm. The mayor was rushed to USF Medical Center and pronounced dead at ten a.m."

Hud was silent as his mother came to stand next to him. As a young senator's wife, she'd been a protégé of Jackie Kennedy both in politics and fashion. She was still a striking presence in her classic suit and pearls, despite her silver hair. Her influence as the widow of a fifth-generation U.S. senator stretched across both parties, but it was a power she rarely used.

There was a long silence between them, as the news changed to the weather. She had to know what he wanted and how important it was to him, to the McCloud legacy.

When his mother didn't speak, Hud smoothed his tie, cleared his throat and said quietly, "This is just what I've been looking for."

His mother gave him a sharp look. "Another chance for you to be hurt?"

"It's what I want." It's what he had to do. Hud muted the volume. He'd turned out to be the screwup in the McCloud family, not Samuel. How in the hell had that happened?

"You excel at running McCloud, Inc." A clothing conglomerate Hud's great-great-grandfather had founded. "Any other man would try to be satisfied with the way things turned out."

"But not a McCloud." McClouds didn't give up. His father had taught him that, along with duty before personal goals.

She sighed heavily. They both knew Hudson had sacrificed his own dreams for the sake of the family.

"I know the public thinks I failed." These last words came out gruffly despite Hud's resolve not to care what anyone else thought. He cleared his throat again. "But I can make it right this time." Hud wanted his mother to be able to hold her head up once more, wanted to hear her laugh with unbridled joy rather than polite response.

"Mayor of San Francisco? The party would be foolish to consider you."

And Hud was a fool to believe he had a chance. Still, he had one card left to play. "They won't turn me down if you ask them. No one refuses Vivian McCloud."

"ROSIE, YOU HAVE two calls waiting." Rosie DeWitt's assistant, Marsha, stuck her head in Rosie's office. "Line one is Walter O'Connell."

Just hours after the mayor's death, the news media and political world was in a frenzy over who was going to run in the election to replace him. Since Rosie was one of Walter's political strategists, he probably wanted her opinion. He might even want her to run the campaign for the Democratic candidate.

"Line two is Casey's daycare."

Anxiety pulsed through Rosie's veins. She set down her coffee and pushed the button for line two. "Is Casey okay?"

"He's fine, Ms. DeWitt." Rosie recognized the voice of Rainbow Daycare's principal, Ms. Phan. Casey attended the Rainbow center after school and during the holidays. "I just wanted to make sure we get our school play on your calendar in late January."

Ouch. She'd missed the last play when Walter had asked Rosie to accompany him to Washington, D.C., to evaluate several candidates for office. She glanced at a photo of her and Casey from last summer. Heads close, they had the same black curly hair, dark brown eyes and energetic grins. Was she letting him down as Ms. Phan always seemed to imply? Sometimes Rosie felt as if she were trying to sail the SS Motherhood beneath the Golden Gate Bridge without a working rudder. No matter how hard she tried to be a good mother, life seemed to conspire against her.

Rosie dutifully penciled the play on her calendar and assured Ms. Phan she'd be there this time.

"And I'm sure you won't be late tonight to pick up Casey. It *is* New Year's Eve." Ms. Phan seemed unable to resist adding, "Once parents begin picking up their children Casey becomes a clock watcher."

To her credit, Rosie didn't snap a pencil or a sharp

retort. She did, however, reach for her coffee. Just holding the warm ceramic mug settled her nerves.

Planning strategy, drafting legislation and writing speeches for candidates and incumbents often meant Rosie was late to pick up her kindergartener. She'd learned to leave money in her budget for the late fees she incurred from Rainbow on a weekly basis. What she hadn't completely mastered was the art of filtering all the advice she received about parenting without taking offense or feeling as if she and Casey needed to go to counseling. They were doing the best they could.

Rosie told Ms. Phan she'd be there before five o'clock closing, then paused to take a sip of coffee before she shifted back to professional mode.

Pressing the button for line one took her to California's power player. "Walter, how are you?" She caught the dinosaur Democrat in mid-cough. He was currently serving as the chairman of the Democratic Party for California. With Walter's approval—and increasingly Rosie's—candidates were groomed by the party for various positions throughout the state.

"A day short of the grave, as usual. Can't seem to shake this cough," he grumbled. "How's it feel to be a backup singer for Senator Alsace?"

"I'm just biding my time until the next political race."

"Ha! Your search for the right candidate is over. Win this one and you can write your own ticket."

"You're going to run for office?" Even as Rosie joked, she was intrigued. Deals were how the American political system worked and how those involved got ahead.

Walter chuckled, a gruff sound that dissolved into another fit of coughing. "Perhaps you've noticed that San Francisco needs a new mayor."

"There's an opening for a squeaky clean candidate with aspirations of glory." Rosie fidgeted in her seat, excited by the prospect of something new. "Who did you have in mind?"

"You win this one, Rosie, and you'll have a shot on the presidential campaign."

"Who?"

"Hudson McCloud."

Rosie looked at the picture of her son again. The McClouds were the California equivalent of the Kennedys. Media followed their every step. Anyone who worked for the McClouds would receive the same scrutiny, and Rosie was fiercely protective of her privacy. She had to turn Walter down.

And yet, part of her yearned for the challenge. Pundits had dismissed Hudson McCloud's career. The campaign would make national news and, possibly, a strategist's career as well. She would just have to work that much harder at keeping her professional life separate from her life with Casey.

"Rosie? Rosie, don't play games with me, girl. You won't get another chance like this anytime soon."

"I don't doubt that." Had Walter lost his mind? Had she? Rosie couldn't quell her curiosity. "Why me?"

"Because you excel at advancing the underdog. Because you don't sugarcoat things." Walter coughed. "And because Vivian McCloud requested you."

* * * * *

Set in darkness beyond the ordinary world.
Passionate tales of life and death.
With characters' lives ruled by laws the everyday
world can't begin to imagine.

n●cturne

It's time to discover the Raintree trilogy...

New York Times bestselling author
LINDA HOWARD
brings you the dramatic first book
RAINTREE: INFERNO

The Ansara Wizards are rising and the Raintree
clan must rejoin the battle against their foes,
testing their powers, relationships and forcing upon
them lives they never could have imagined before...

Turn the page for a sneak preview
of the captivating first book
in the Raintree trilogy,
RAINTREE: INFERNO by LINDA HOWARD
On sale April 25.

Dante Raintree stood with his arms crossed as he watched the woman on the monitor. The image was in black and white to better show details; color distracted the brain. He focused on her hands, watching every move she made, but what struck him most was how uncommonly *still* she was. She didn't fidget or play with her chips, or look around at the other players. She peeked once at her down card, then didn't touch it again, signaling for another hit by tapping a fingernail on the table. Just because she didn't seem to be paying attention to the other players, though, didn't mean she was as unaware as she seemed.

"What's her name?" Dante asked.

"Lorna Clay," replied his chief of security, Al Rayburn.

"At first I thought she was counting, but she doesn't pay enough attention."

"She's paying attention, all right," Dante murmured. "You just don't see her doing it." A card

counter had to remember every card played. Supposedly counting cards was impossible with the number
of decks used by the casinos, but there were those
rare individuals who could calculate the odds even
with multiple decks.

"I thought that, too," said Al. "But look at this
piece of tape coming up. Someone she knows comes
up to her and speaks, she looks around and starts
chatting, completely misses the play of the people to
her left—and doesn't look around even when the
deal comes back to her, just taps that finger. And
damn if she didn't win. Again."

Dante watched the tape, rewound it, watched it
again. Then he watched it a third time. There had to
be something he was missing, because he couldn't
pick out a single giveaway.

"If she's cheating," Al said with something like
respect, "she's the best I've ever seen."

"What does your gut say?"

Al scratched the side of his jaw, considering.
Finally, he said, "If she isn't cheating, she's the
luckiest person walking. She wins. Week in, week
out, she wins. Never a huge amount, but I ran the
numbers and she's into us for about five grand a
week. Hell, boss, on her way out of the casino she'll
stop by a slot machine, feed a dollar in and walk
away with at least fifty. It's never the same machine,
either. I've had her watched, I've had her followed,

I've even looked for the same faces in the casino every time she's in here, and I can't find a common denominator."

"Is she here now?"

"She came in about half an hour ago. She's playing blackjack, as usual."

"Bring her to my office," Dante said, making a swift decision. "Don't make a scene."

"Got it," said Al, turning on his heel and leaving the security center.

Dante left, too, going up to his office. His face was calm. Normally he would leave it to Al to deal with a cheater, but he was curious. How was she doing it? There were a lot of bad cheaters, a few good ones, and every so often one would come along who was the stuff of which legends were made: the cheater who didn't get caught, even when people were alert and the camera was on him—or, in this case, her.

It was possible to simply be lucky, as most people understood luck. Chance could turn a habitual loser into a big-time winner. Casinos, in fact, thrived on that hope. But luck itself wasn't habitual, and he knew that what passed for luck was often something else: cheating. And there was the other kind of luck, the kind he himself possessed, but it depended not on chance but on who and what he was. He knew it was an innate power and not Dame Fortune's erratic smile. Since power like his was rare, the odds made it likely the woman he'd been watching was merely a very clever cheat.

Her skill could provide her with a very good living, he thought, doing some swift calculations in his head. Five grand a week equaled $260,000 a year, and that was just from his casino. She probably hit them all, careful to keep the numbers relatively low so she stayed under the radar.

He wondered how long she'd been taking him, how long she'd been winning a little here, a little there, before Al noticed.

The curtains were open on the wall-to-wall window in his office, giving the impression, when one first opened the door, of stepping out onto a covered balcony. The glazed window faced west, so he could catch the sunsets. The sun was low now, the sky painted in purple and gold. At his home in the mountains, most of the windows faced east, affording him views of the sunrise. Something in him needed both the greeting and the goodbye of the sun. He'd always been drawn to sunlight, maybe because fire was his element to call, to control.

He checked his internal time: four minutes until sundown. Without checking the sunrise tables every day, he knew exactly when the sun would slide behind the mountains. He didn't own an alarm clock. He didn't need one. He was so acutely attuned to the sun's position that he had only to check within himself to know the time. As for waking at a particular time, he was one of those people who could tell himself to wake at a certain time, and he did. That talent had nothing to do with being Raintree, so he didn't have to hide it; a lot of perfectly ordinary people had the same ability.

He had other talents and abilities, however, that did require careful shielding. The long days of summer instilled in him an almost sexual high, when he could feel contained power buzzing just beneath his skin. He had to be doubly careful not to cause candles to leap into flame just by his presence, or to start wildfires with a glance in the dry-as-tinder brush. He loved Reno; he didn't want to burn it down. He just felt so damn *alive* with all the sunshine pouring down that he wanted to let the energy pour through him instead of holding it inside.

This must be how his brother Gideon felt while pulling lightning, all that hot power searing through his muscles, his veins. They had this in common, the connection with raw power. All the members of the far-flung Raintree clan had some power, some heightened ability, but only members of the royal family could channel and control the earth's natural energies.

Dante wasn't just of the royal family, he was the Dranir, the leader of the entire clan. "Dranir" was synonymous with king, but the position he held wasn't ceremonial, it was one of sheer power. He was the oldest son of the previous Dranir, but he would have been passed over for the position if he hadn't also inherited the power to hold it.

Behind him came Al's distinctive knock on the door. The outer office was empty, Dante's secretary having gone home hours before. "Come in," he called, not turning from his view of the sunset.

The door opened, and Al said, "Mr. Raintree, this is Lorna Clay."

Dante turned and looked at the woman, all his senses on alert. The first thing he noticed was the vibrant color of her hair, a rich, dark red that encompassed a multitude of shades from copper to burgundy. The warm amber light danced along the iridescent strands, and he felt a hard tug of sheer lust in his gut. Looking at her hair was almost like looking at fire, and he had the same reaction.

The second thing he noticed was that she was spitting mad.

nocturne™

IT'S TIME TO DISCOVER
THE RAINTREE TRILOGY...

There have always been those among us
who are more than human...

Don't miss the dramatic first book by
New York Times bestselling author

LINDA
HOWARD

Raintree:
Inferno

On sale May.

Raintree: Haunted by Linda Winstead Jones
Available June.

Raintree: Sanctuary by Beverly Barton
Available July.

Romantic SUSPENSE

**Sparked by Danger,
Fueled by Passion.**

*This month and every month look for
four new heart-racing romances
set against a backdrop of suspense!*

Available in May 2007

Safety in Numbers
(Wild West Bodyguards miniseries)
by Carla Cassidy

Jackson's Woman
by Maggie Price

Shadow Warrior
(Night Guardians miniseries)
by Linda Conrad

One Cool Lawman
by Diane Pershing

Available wherever you buy books!

COMING NEXT MONTH

#1416 THE BEST-KEPT SECRET • Melinda Curtis
Singles…with Kids
What if your son's grandmother calls, wanting your help? The problem? The woman doesn't know she's a grandmother. Rosie DeWitt is given the career opportunity of a lifetime—campaign manager for Hudson McCloud. But Hudson and his mother have no idea Rosie had a child with Hudson's brother. And she wants to keep it that way.

#1417 SAFE IN HIS ARMS • Kay David
Count on a Cop
Daniel Bishop is a cop. And a good one. Which is why he never expects to fall in love with a suspect in his latest case.

#1418 THE WRONG MAN FOR HER • Kathryn Shay
Going Back
She still loves him desperately, even though he once broke her heart. But Nick hasn't changed at all, which means that now he's back, Madelyn has to stay as far away from him as she can. The problem is she's his new boss, so how far can she actually get?

#1419 HER SISTER'S CHILD • Cynthia Thomason
A Little Secret
When you want something badly enough, seems you'll do just about anything to get it. And Julia Sommerville wants custody of her sister's daughter about as much as she's ever wanted anything…even if it might mean losing the man she's fallen in love with—for the second time.

#1420 SMALL-TOWN FAMILY • Margaret Watson
It seemed to Charlotte that Dylan's quest to find his real father would destroy the only family she'd ever known. And so she did what she thought she had to do to protect herself. Would the man she loved ever be able to forgive her?

#1421 IT TAKES TWO • Joanne Michael
Single Father
It's hard enough being a single dad, but when your bright young daughter is struggling after losing her mom, it can also be heartbreaking. So when Marc Doucette encounters Abby Miller and she offers to help, he thinks she's a gift from above. It's the heated glances and stolen kisses between Marc and Abby he's not sure he's ready for.

HSRCNM0407